AM

To Dona[l]

D1098679

Fiction Gift Aid
£

0 029310 028511

Not Ready

A COLLECTION OF STORIES ~~ABOUT CHILDHOOD~~

Best wishes,

Robob Sift.

22.01.22

by
Robert Swift

Grosvenor House
Publishing Limited

20 Crossland Crescent, Peebles
EH45 8LF

This book is published by
Grosvenor House Publishing Ltd
Link House
140 The Broadway, Tolworth, Surrey, KT6 7HT.
www.grosvenorhousepublishing.co.uk

This book is a work of fiction. Any resemblance to
people or events, past or present, is purely coincidental.

A CIP record for this book
is available from the British Library

ISBN 978-1-83975-804-1

for Franny

About the Author

A father of four, Robert Swift has spent nearly all of his working life as a social worker working with vulnerable children. Over the years he has found some time to write. A number of his short stories have been published and some have won prizes. He has written two books of non-fiction: *The Family Business*, published by the British Association of Adoption and Fostering, which is a personalised account of the adoption process published under a pseudonym, and *Adopting a Child in Scotland*, a handbook about adoption, published by CoramBAAF and now in its second edition. Robert has also written a number of newspaper features about child care and adoption.

Preface

The author has seen at first hand how children's life-chances are affected by poverty in all its forms. He has observed the enduring impact of early trauma on the development of children and he has been struck about by how the care system fails many children and indeed compounds the neglect and abuse suffered by some. Children who have experienced adversity can suffer the impact throughout their lives. But vulnerable children can triumph when given the care and support they need. Adopted and Looked After children have achieved high office in government, have become national poets and sporting heroes. And there are countless numbers who have become unsung heroes; turning out to be great parents themselves, or just being good people, getting on with their lives and making the world a better place.

This collection of short stories tries to tell what it can be like to be a child, a young person or a parent in Britain today. Some of the stories seek to expose the *system* that lets children down. Others touch on the remarkable resilience and compassion of children. Some look at the funny side of family life.

We often hear the phrase *children are our future* and indeed they are our most precious resource. Children are remarkable for their wisdom, their passion to change the world for the better, their resilience and their sense of what is right and wrong. In a fairer world where all children have the chance to reach their potential we would have no fears for the future.

All the characters in these stories are wholly fictitious.

Ali Smith has written of one of the stories, *The Gift,* *"I guarantee you will never forget... The Gift."*

Prologue

The first story in this collection, *Home*, looks at the plight of a young asylum-seeker and the friendship he finds with a young person in care. The next story, *The Gift*, explores what it is like to foster a traumatised child and the struggle of the foster care family to understand her bizarre behaviour. *More Storage Space* is a humorous account of an only child's search for meaning and his frustrations with parents who seem to have been born in the wrong century. *Silver for Good Luck* is about a newborn baby whose future is uncertain and *Spaghetti Junction* is a light-hearted look at the impact of impending empty-nest syndrome. *The Light of the World* looks at domestic abuse and a mother's hopeless love for her child. *The Plaited Dog Turd with the Oak Leaf Sail* is a mysterious tale about a man on the edge and *Learning the Moves* is about the search for an adoptive family for a brother and sister, which challenges the old stereotypes of adoption. *The Orange Buoy* looks at love and loss and *Susie's Song* tells of the emotional complexities of an inter-country adoption.

The Taxidermist is about a young carer with additional needs and *Security* is about the former pupil of a residential school trying to make sense of his traumatic time there, with a whodunnit question left hanging at the end. *Gold* tells of a young person who disappears from her family and ends with a big surprise for her parents and *Three for a Girl* is a tragic story about stillbirth. *Not Ready for Love* looks at the agony of being a teenager in love with the unattainable and *Family Man* is a very short story that speaks for itself. *The Bogeyman* is a cautionary tale about a disintegrating family and *The Exorcism* tells of a chance meeting between a woman and a boy who helps her in an unusual quest. *Evensong* looks at the clash between contrasting worlds and the last story, *Fishing*, is a simple tale about a father and son's time together.

Contents

1

Lost in the Crowd

'Thae pigeons've got it wrong.'

'I'm sorry? Excuse me, Joey?'

'You talk weird, Farid.'

'You keep telling me this, Joey. I am trying. You are helping me very much.'

The sun is shining with a rare warmth. The two figures lean against a lime tree, part of an avenue that has stood for more than a century, maybe two. Walkers in summer cotton and cyclists in shorts are enjoying being amongst the stippled shadows of the great trees, anchored like rocks, their roots stretching deep into the earth and their trembling leaves touching the sky.

'Listen, just listen to them, man, will you?'

They lift their eyes, searching and listening. There is a silence; the pigeons don't cooperate.

'I don't understand.'

'Hold on Farid. Music has to include the rests as well you know, the silences?'

After a moment one starts: crooing its simple line.

'There, you see,' says Joey triumphantly: 'Croo oo oo oo, croo oo oo oo, croo oo oo oo, *croo*.' He copies the line in an undulating song, with a voice that still holds the pitch of a child.

Farid looks at his friend. 'I hear the song of the doves, but what you want me to say?'

'They're pigeons, Farid. Doves is white. They get released at weddings and stuff. It's just not finished off properly, the song. Can you not hear? There's an extra croo at the end. It's obvious. It should go Croo oo oo oo, croo oo oo oo, croo, oo, oo, oo. Finish. It's too messy with the extra croo at the end. Specially the way it lifts like that. It's a mistake, it must be. At first I thought it was just the one pigeon that had got it wrong, but if you listen you'll hear that they all dae it. Can you not hear?'

'I hear these birds all over. Even in my home town they sing.'

'And do they have that extra croo in Syria, or wherever you say you're from?'

'Joey, I am sorry, I never observed such things.' He is transported back to the street where he lived, the dust everywhere, the walk to get water and the queue for bread, the men who threatened his family and wanted him to join in the fight, the disappearance of his father and the memory of his mother rocking backwards and forwards in her armchair, still covered in plastic to keep

2

it nice. The house is darkened by blankets nailed up against the shattered windows.

'I'm beginning to think, Farid, that you've nae music in you; nae soul.'

Farid looks at Joey blankly.

It's lunchtime and the path is busy. It's a day to make everyone feel glad to be alive. Joey and Farid have a good pitch. They have got to know one or two faces over the last couple of days. A passing nurse drops a fifty p into their polystyrene cup with a smile.

'Cheers missus.' Joey has a cheeky grin that endears him to donors. Farid's olive skin and good looks also help. They have a productive partnership.

'I wonder if they learn it or if it's in their genes.'

'Excuse me Joey?'

'The pigeons. I mean, I wonder if the ones in Africa, or England even, sound the same, or if it's a Scottish thing; that it's just the Scottish ones that cannae sing properly. I bet that's it. I wish you'd paid more attention, Farid, back in Syria. This could be an important discovery. We could go and find out. A research trip round Europe.'

'Excuse me, Joey, what you mean? About the jeans?'

'You know: genes: G.E.N.E.S. Biology, National Five.'

'I don't understand. I don't think we have such things in my country.'

Joey rolls his eyes and shakes his head.

A woman is coming towards them. She crosses the cycle lane without looking and a man freewheeling down the hill in bright lycra and a seriously streamlined helmet rings his bell and has to break and turn. He twists his head with a shout, but it's as if she hasn't heard him. To the boys she seems very old. She sashays closer, her red pleated skirt stirring and swaying about her legs. Despite the heat she is wearing a cardigan buttoned to the neck. It too is red, as is the headscarf, tied with a knot at the back of her head. She is carrying a basket.

'Watch out, here comes Red Riding Hood's granny.' Joey grins at Farid, who looks puzzled.

'I've been watching you two,' she says, her head nodding slightly. Her false teeth are stained red from her lipstick. 'You shouldn't be doing this. Why don't you go home?'

'Nae home to go to missus,' says Joey. 'I was in a children's home but they chucked me out.'

She raises an eyebrow, still nodding; it's a condition she has. 'I'm not stupid, young man. And I'm not giving you money, because you'll just spend it on drink and drugs.'

Joey begins to protest. 'Hey now, missus, just wait..'

She cuts him off, shuttering her eyes for a moment behind her thin flickering lids. 'I don't want to know; but here, you can have these.' She reaches into her basket and draws out a couple of packs of shop-bought sandwiches. 'And you'd do well to look at this,' she says, producing a bible. She puts it carefully down beside the polystyrene cup and straightening up, looks at them severely for a moment, still nodding, before turning away. She's heavily scented, and an artificial fragrance of impossible flowers lingers after she's moved off. Joey grabs his throat with both hands as if choking and makes a guttural gurgling sound. He giggles like a child, and rolls backwards on his buttocks till he's lying on his back, laughing out loud with his legs kicking the air.

'Off her heid.' If she hears them she shows no sign. Another cyclist has to break and swerve to avoid her.

They unwrap the sandwiches. Ham and salad. Farid says he isn't hungry.

'You'll fade away Farid my man if you dinnae eat more.'

'You remember I do not eat ham, Joey.'

'But you could have the bread at least,' says Joey, but Farid shakes his head.

There is a silence between them while Joey eats. It's comfortable in the sunshine. 'We're very lucky you know,' says Joey.

'I beg your pardon, Joey, in what way we are lucky?'

'You and me Farid are lucky because we've got more than the average number of legs.'

Farid frowns. He often finds it difficult to follow Joey's train of thought; he has a habit of coming out

5

with unexpected facts and ideas. 'I'm sorry Joey, I don't understand you again.'

'Think about it, Farid my man. We've both got two legs. Some poor buggers dinnae have two legs, you know, like if they've had one amputated, or even both. So by the law of averages that means we've got more than the average number. Taking the planet as a whole that is.'

There is no disputing Joey's logic but Farid queries his conclusions about luck. 'Maybe it is they who have lost their legs who are *unlucky*, Joey. Everyone should have a right to have their legs.' There is a crack in his voice.

'It's a funny thought, though, don't you think? That because a few buggers have lost their legs we have more than the average number. And eyes and hands and balls come to that. I feel lucky even if you don't. Though maybe folk would give us a bit more money if we had a limb or two missing.' He ruminates for a time, then belches and gets to his feet. 'Hey, maybe we could pretend? I could strap you up so you just have the one leg that folk can see. How about that, Farid, eh?' Joey has a broad grim. He grins a lot. 'We could make a fortune.'

But Farid doesn't see the funny side. He explodes with rage in a way Joey has never seen. His face is red and his eyes are wet with a wild desperation. 'Joey, you don't know anything. You know nothing at all about luck or about the world. I know people without legs, Joey. I have seen people without legs.' He stands up and paces about. 'I have seen people bleed to death because of the bombs and because there is no-one to help them and the blood just comes and comes. Children and old people who have done no wrong to anyone. And their mothers weep and their brothers cry out with anger and go and die in a hopeless fight that no-one can win.' He is crying and his shouting makes passers-by turn their heads to see what the commotion is about. Joey is looking at him with his mouth open. 'You know nothing Joey. And there is no pain relief; there is no comfort, no god, nothing to give hope. And children cry out and their cries get quieter till they give up, till they die, and their mothers weep and their fathers bury them in the dust and the rocks and wait for the next attack.' He kicks the sandwich wrappers. He wanders into the cycle lane and a cyclist shouts at him. Joey's grin has disappeared. They look into each other's eyes for a moment and then Farid turns and begins to run. He's been running for two years.

'Hey, wait on there, Farid,' shouts Joey taking after him.

They leave an empty space. Empty except for the sandwich wrappers and the open bible; its texts fluttering in the breeze. Soon the pigeons gather and peck at the crumbs, their heads jerking as they squabble and flap to avoid the passing feet, with no time for song.

*

Joey and Farid's paths had first crossed in the children's home. Joey had been there for a couple of years since his foster care placement broke down. Farid had been found on the A1, wandering around in the early hours. He'd told them he had been in a lorry for weeks; that he was from Syria and had to get out because his life was in danger. He said his father was dead and that he came over with an uncle, but got separated some time back and was now on his own. He said he was fifteen, but he looked older. People were suspicious about his story and about his age. They thought he had been coached. He was being *assessed*.

When he was first taken to the children's home Farid took his meals in his room and watched television all day long. The staff checked on him from time to time. He was usually asleep or pretending to be. He kept his light on all night. He ventured downstairs one day but two of the young people were fighting about something and cups were being thrown around in the kitchen. One smashed against the wall near where he stood in the doorway. A fragment spun round at his feet like a piece of shrapnel. Farid went back to his room and blocked the door with a chest of drawers.

The staff kept trying to coax him out, but it was Joey to whom he responded. Joey had a way about him that you couldn't help liking. Soon the two of them were out and about and Joey was introducing Farid to Scottish life. Joey told Farid things, like the whole population of the world could fit into Loch Ness with space to spare.

'What is Lock Ness?'

'It's Loch, Farid, Loch. Use the back of your throat. You never heard of Loch Ness? I'll take you one day. We could look for the monster. You must have heard of Nessie?'

Joey told him that the oldest trees on earth were bristle-cone pines which were five thousand years old. It took two and a half thousand years for light to reach earth from Andromeda, the closest galaxy. 'You can see it with the naked eye. I'll show you.' They went into the garden one night to look, but there was too much cloud and light pollution. The air was heavy with the smell from the breweries. 'One day Farid, one day.' said Joey.

Farid didn't give much information away about himself, but Joey didn't seem bothered; he didn't like talking about his family either. The last time he went home he'd let himself in through the back door as usual. 'Hiya, son. There's some tea in the pot.' His mother had been sitting on the sofa watching a soap on the TV. His little sister had cautiously come into the room. Her face was tear-stained and she wanted forgiveness for something. 'Out,' their mother had said, coldly and finally, without looking round, and the girl had broken out into sobs again. Joey had given her a smile and a wink and she'd started coming towards him at a running trot. 'I said out,' her mother had repeated and the girl had stopped, turned and left.

A man had come into the room. He was wearing shorts and a singlet and had a tattooed dragon on his arm. He'd looked at Joey for a second, then he'd gone over to the sofa and, bent over Joey's mother from behind and put his hand inside the front of her Tee-shirt. She'd giggled and shaken him away. He'd taken her cigarette and inhaled a long drag before putting it back between her fingers. 'Joey, this is Kenny,' his mother had said, without taking her eyes off the soap. He'd signalled to Joey with a jerk of his head to follow him to the kitchen. Once there he'd closed the door. 'Listen, pal,' he'd said. 'Don't get any ideas. There's no room for you here, see? So you just drink your tea and fuck off again, okay?' He'd leaned against the door frame with his thumb tucked into the waistband of his shorts.

*

It's a few days since Joey and Farid last saw each other. Joey is on a slip road, hitching a lift back home. *Home.* The word gives him no comfort. He's been to Glasgow but it didn't work out. He spent the previous night in a stairwell, the shadows thrown about by a yellow flickering candle he'd got hold of. He needs money. There wasn't a lot in the paper cup today and what there was got taken by a couple of guys he didn't want to argue with, so he's got nothing. They took his phone too. It's raining and his hair has got slicked down like greasy feathers around his head.

A car pulls up, the orange neon from the overhead lights slipping over its dark silky body. He opens the door and puts his head inside. There's no interior light, but the car's warm and there's a gentle throb of bass music. After a moment he climbs in and sinks into the creaking leather seat.

'All right, son? Good to be out the rain eh?' The car pulls out and they are soon speeding along in the fast lane of the M8. 'There are some cans and smokes in the back if you fancy them?'

'No, you're all right,' says Joey looking through the side window at the miles passing in a blurr. He thinks about Farid and wonders what has become of him. He had chased after him the day they fell out, but he'd lost sight of him in the winding streets. He hasn't been back to the children's home. Couldn't face it. He wonders if Farid is there.

They enter the outskirts of the city and the car pulls up at some traffic lights. The driver puts his hand on Joey's knee, but he jerks his leg away. 'Fuck off,' he snaps.

'Okay son, okay,' says the driver.

The window has become steamed up and Joey wipes it with his sleeve.

'Bit of a smell if you don't mind me saying,' says the driver, 'although I quite like it.' He puts the car in gear, anticipating that the lights are about to change. Joey quickly reaches for the door handle and bolts out of the car.

'Hey, hang on there, son,' shouts the driver. He makes a grab and catches hold of Joey's jacket, but he manages to pull away and turns to the driver through the pouring rain. 'I'm not your fucking son,' he says, and he slams the car door. The lights turn green and the car behind sounds its horn.

'You little bastard,' shouts the driver as he pulls away and Joey runs into the darkness.

*

Farid is sitting on a bench in the gardens that run along Princes Street. He and Joey used to come here. There is a little brass plate to the memory of someone called Pamela. She must have been special, he thinks, *loved*. David Livingstone stands above him; a modest statue; blackened, but tinged with green. He knows a bit about Livingstone from Joey. Joey collects knowledge the way iron filings are drawn to a magnet. Farther away is the Scott Monument, like a monstrous dirty wedding cake decoration. Farid has never heard of Walter Scott and wonders if he fought slavery too. Given the size of his monument he must have been a greater man than

Livingstone, he surmises. But Scott looks like a tired clerk, whereas Livingstone has a lion skin draped around him and holds a book, his finger keeping his place. He has a gun, a stick and a leather bag slung over his shoulder. The monument reads simply LIVINGSTONE. The passers-by pay no attention to the great man, who Farid knows as a friend to the oppressed. Farid has had direct experience of slavery. He needs a hero. The statue stands at an angle, looking towards Morrison's and Accessorize; it is smeared with gull excrement.

'All right there Farid?' Joey sits down next to him.

'It's good to see you man,' says Farid, beaming broadly. 'But you do not look good. Where have you been?'

'Oh here and there, Farid mate, here and there.' He leans forward, rubbing his hands together. They are quiet for a few moments, just enjoying being next to each other.

'I'm sorry, Joey,' says Farid. 'I have missed you.'

'Me too, Farid boy.'

They sit quietly, both looking at Livingstone, whose fixed gaze is on the shoppers.

'Here's a thing, Farid. Did you know that more people get killed by falling coconuts than are killed by sharks? What do you think of that?'

Farid looks at him and smiles. 'I think Joey that you are very wise and I am glad you are my friend. I have something to say to you, Joey; something very good, I hope you will agree. I have traced my uncle and the authorities are giving him a flat in a place called Dundee. You must come and live with us, Joey. To our new home. You will be part of our family. We can all look after each other. You will like my uncle and I know he will like you.'

Joey returns his smile. 'Aye. Maybe. We could carry on with the pigeon study.' They are quiet for a while. Then Joey says, 'Hey, do you want to go and see something?

'What is that Joey?'

'There's a lamb with two heids in the museum.'

Farid smiles. 'Yes, why not?' They get to their feet and are soon lost in the crowd of shoppers and sightseers that throng Princes Street.

2

The Gift

The railings are set in the top of a low stone wall, and by clinging to them with her hands she can stay off the ground. She works her way round the wall; hand over hand and foot over foot. It's a tricky operation; if she falls off she'll be swallowed up by the swamp, sucked down into dark oblivion. Her hands are cold and her coat is undone. She has conversations with herself, partly out loud and partly locked up tight inside herself. There are various gaps in the wall; at the school gates for instance, where she becomes cocooned in a protective membrane, and floats like a bubble to the next section. A group of other children are chanting something at her, but she doesn't hear them. The school bell goes and everyone disappears. Miss Clark crosses the playground and comes up to her with her hand outstretched. Come on Becky, the bell's gone. Oh dear, have you had an accident? Never mind, come on, let's go and sort you out. They head off for the toilets together.

Janice

We always wanted to be foster parents. Foster *carers* they call us these days. I don't know why exactly, we just wanted to look after kids, needed to maybe, though the social workers don't like you to say that. It's the most important thing you can do, isn't it, bringing up kids, and you get such a kick out of it when things go well, you know, when they begin to really talk to you, or stop wetting the bed or whatever. But we never imagined anyone like Becky. We'd had a couple of placements before, but nothing really *testing*. That's another word they like to use. When the social worker phoned us she was desperate; Becky was in the office with her things in one of those black bin liners. I can picture her now with her head down, not speaking to anyone. Her foster placement had broken down and they needed somewhere that night. You know what they're like: If you could even take her for the night Janice, just to give us a breathing space... What can you say? She soils a bit they said. A touch of understatement there, I'd say. Some days Becky has to change her pants twenty times. She smears it on the bedroom wall, she shits in bed ('scuse my language, you become kind of immune after a while) and doesn't tell anyone, she shits on the landing and on the floor of the bathroom, and you stand in it and spread it about before you know what's happening. She hides her soiled pants in drawers and under pillows, even in the cistern. It can take a while to track down the smell. We've had five months of this so far.

*

Who knows what Becky thinks. Not that she's a quiet girl; she chatters away and on some days can seem like any other child, except that it can be difficult to follow the thread. And when you ask her why she has hidden her pants in the cistern she puts her head down and won't speak. Maybe she doesn't know, though it can seem a bit hard to believe. She's ten years old and this is her eighth foster placement. She's been home once or twice in between times, but it hasn't worked out. She's desperate to be with her mother, but her mother doesn't believe the allegations, so there's not much chance of that.

She could be quite pretty if she took more care of herself, but she doesn't seem to care. It's as if she wants to repel people. Her long black hair had to be cut off because she wouldn't brush it, and kept pulling it over her eyes. And of course she smells. The walking toilet, the children call her at school, and she's got no friends. She gets really upset about it at times, but doesn't do anything about it. If she'd just went to the toilet and kept herself clean.

John

Becky's okay. It's quite funny at times. Our toilet is at the top of the stairs, and when she first came here she'd sit on the bog with her legs apart and the door open; she seemed to be waiting for me to find her like that, with a great smile on her face. At first I'd shout for mum. Mum, she's doing it again. And mum would come running up the stairs and say, Now Becky, we've said before, in this house the rule is that we close the door. We've all become very matter of fact about it now. Becky you've forgotten to close the door again. And she is getting a bit better, but it's a slow business. Mind, the word business has a new meaning round here. I don't know where they all come from. It's the ones you come across on the floor that are the worst; she seems to produce them in camouflaged colours, so that even when you're on the lookout you can easy miss them and end up standing in one. Mind even that can have it's funny side. Michelle had a new boyfriend a few weeks ago. A stuck up sort with a stripy tie and a personalised number plate. He said he worked in finance; probably on a supermarket checkout if you ask me. None of us took to him much, and of course that made Michelle all the more keen on him. She brought him back one night after they'd been out. Course he flies upstairs to the bog, straight into one of Becky's strategically placed deposits. He's gone for ages, till Michelle goes looking for him and finds him trying to clean the stuff off his shoes and off the carpet with a bit of bog roll. She tells him it's the cat and not to worry. Not that we've got a cat of course. But then he comes downstairs, you know for a coffee and a snog, and his hand strays under the cushion straight into one of Becky's little parcels of jobby. He was out of it after that; a house of nutters who wrap up cat shite and hide it under the cushions. Michelle was furious. The rest of us had been in bed, but we were soon awake when we heard her screaming at Becky that she'd ruined her life. Becky just sat there on the bed, saying it wasn't me, it wasn't me. Then mum made Michelle apologise to Becky. I told Becky afterwards that we were all well rid of him.

Doug

It's like living with a time bomb. I mean what if she makes some allegations about *me*? Her last foster parents are suspended, but we don't know the full story. She's made allegations about a whole string of folk, you just don't know what to believe. She calls me Uncle Doug. She's just a little girl, but at the same time she's not a child; her innocence has gone, and you can't put it back. It's not something you can let yourself think about; I mean what must have happened to her. And that boyfriend of her mother hasn't even been charged. Who'd believe Becky, standing up in court? Every other sentence she utters is a lie. She'd probably just stand there not saying anything, with her head down, trying to pull her hair over her face to hide from it all. But everyone knows he did it. Sometimes I think to myself if the chance arose; if I came across him in a deserted street I'd teach him. And her useless mother just stands by him; she's chosen him and to hell with Becky. And the number of times she comes to visit Becky and she's got a black eye. Poor Woman. What can she do?

Michelle

I've tried with Becky, but I just can't get through. I don't care what they say, I think she shites deliberately. She must know what she's doing when she hides her pants under her pillow and smears the stuff on the walls. There are times, little spells of a few days, when she's normal; it's heaven, and we all say how great she is and clever, and then, just when you think it might be safe to bring your boyfriend home, it starts again, and it can be ten times as worse as before, or that's how it feels after a break. I can't understand it, it must be deliberate. We have these family meetings now where we talk about it; how we all care about Becky and want to help her with this problem. Sometimes I think she just needs a good smack. It's amazing how mum keeps so patient with her. If you ask me all these therapists have weakened her brain and she's got no common sense left. She used to give us the odd clip when we were kids and it never did us any harm.

Janice

Becky does these drawings during her therapy sessions. Lots of red, with people in fires or drowning, and always pictures of the family, with herself on the outside, and dad as a monster figure. It's obvious really, isn't it? She has no control; its a reflex action, like blushing, she just can't help it. The therapist says it's like when you're so angry you just blow, you can't help it. I still don't understand it properly. They tell us that the shit is maybe a way of protecting herself. Perhaps he won't do it if I'm dirty and unattractive. Apparently, sometimes the excrement is part of the actual abuse. There's a whole seedy world out there that we have no idea about. God knows what you'd find if you lifted the roofs off some of these houses.

The worst time was probably a couple of months ago. It had all got on top of us, to the point that Michelle was going to leave home. There seemed to be no end in sight, though everyone said we were doing a great job, if we could just hang on in there. The four of us had a talk, and decided we needed to get away together without Becky; a normal weekend together. So they arranged some respite for Becky with some other foster carers, and off she went without a backward glance. We all stayed in this little cottage in Robin Hoods Bay. It's a higgledy piggledy sort of place that looks as if its sliding into the sea; pretty, with lots of funny little buildings with hiding places that the smugglers used to lie low in. It didn't work very well. I couldn't stop thinking about Becky. Every time I saw a child or a pile of dog dirt, and even when I didn't. I think I drove the rest of them mad. Will you stop talking about Becky they kept saying. And I just couldn't do with sex, haven't been able to for weeks. Poor Doug.

Doug

There was something about the grey misty weather that seemed to get inside us all. Janice could hardly crack her face into a smile; felt guilty as hell for leaving Becky, I suppose. And she tensed up when I tried to give her so much as a cuddle. The kids were great; they seemed to know it was up to them to salvage something. It was as if they went back ten years. John chased Michelle along the beach with a wet bit of seaweed, and she screeched at him, pretending she didn't like it; worried about getting her white jacket dirty. It seemed to do them good; in the bar they got to talking about how things were when they were little. Like lying in bed together waiting for Santa, but falling asleep of course before I came in with the presents. And each of them swearing the next morning that they'd caught a glimpse of him. Then we all looked up at Janice, and she was just crying, and couldn't explain why. She wanted to phone, but I wouldn't let her. I still don't know if she made a call without telling me.

Michelle

The weekend away was a laugh in some ways. John and me became friends again. He's all right really, but I wish he'd do something about his appearance; that ragged old denim jacket and his greasy hair; you can see people looking at him. We got into this thing in one of the gift shops: Have you remembered to take your Valium today, John?, and: When is it you see your probation officer again, John? Mum and Dad didn't think it was very funny, but John and me thought it was great; you should've seen the faces on some of them women.

I suppose it made me realise how important Becky is to Mum. She was so cut up about leaving her. Probably too important, but that's mum. And I suppose we're big enough to look after ourselves now. I just wish she'd stop doing it; she's meant to be very bright.

Janice

She didn't make one mistake when we were away. We brought her some fossils back that we'd bought in a little shop. And she gave me a present. She gave me a real hug and a kiss and gave me this beautifully wrapped gift, all done up with Christmas paper and ribbons she'd found somewhere. She was so excited she wanted to help me undo it. There were several layers of paper all carefully sellotaped up. We had to get the scissors. I don't know why I was surprised really; she obviously thought I'd be genuinely pleased. Inside the parcel was a lump of shite, carefully wrapped in several layers of toilet roll.

3

More Storage Space

Logan's parents wondered if his moods might be connected with Mrs. Brown's death. His facial spots seemed to be responding to the lotion Beth had bought, so it couldn't be those. She and Mike talk in whispers, even when Logan is out, standing together at the sink, looking out onto the neatly clipped square of lawn with its whirligig centrepiece, revolving steadily with a pegged mixture of limp underwear, tired looking T-shirts and stiff white bath towels. The grass is surrounded by weedless borders of colourful, spiky dahlias whose tubers Mike has lovingly watched over during their sleep through the cheerless winter months in trays in the attic.

'Look good don't they, love?' Mike is washing, as always, and Beth is drying using a linen tea towel printed with Wordsworth's Dove cottage: a souvenir from their last holiday.

'What's that Mike?'

'The dahlias. I was saying they look good.' He puts another plate onto the drainer and it is immediately snatched up by Beth, who works faster than Mike.

'Yes lovely Mike, but I wish you wouldn't go off at tangents like that. I wonder if we need to get a dishwasher; I waste hours waiting for you to wash.' She waits for the next dripping item. 'She was a nice enough woman; very nice,' reasoned Beth, 'but she was eighty-two, and we didn't know her that well, did we? Mind, she always gave Logan a sweet when he delivered her morning paper, and of course, she's been there ever since he was a baby. It must be hard for him, just to go past her house every morning and not leave a paper.' She held a glass up to the light, looking for smears, then glanced into the sink. 'You need to change that water, Mike. What do you think?'

'I thought I'd get this pan clean first, love.'

'Not about the water.' She sighs. 'Really, Mike, I wish you'd keep up. Logan, and his moods?'

'I think it's just his age. Teenagers, you know? Hormones.'

Mike watches him one morning, from under the car boot lid. He's taken an empty cardboard box out to the car, parked on the pink block paved drive, and will shortly take it back inside, still empty. Spying, but in a good cause. But Logan doesn't seem to react as he passes the late Mrs Brown's gate. He seems to be reading a copy of *The Sun* before pushing it through the McFadyens' letter box. Mike wonders if it might be page three.

'Nice Dahlias, Mike.' Mike jumps as if caught in the act of something illicit, and bangs his head on the edge of the hatchback door.

'Thanks, Rob', he replies to his neighbour, 'you should see the ones in the back,' but Rob has already passed out of earshot.

'He's deep,' Beth says that night, as they sip their Pinot Grigiot during the ten o'clock news. 'And he's bright. Remember what they said about him at parents' evening? It goes together.'

'What?'

'Being deep and bright. He's got a creative talent. That self-portrait he did in art was so...brooding.'

'Hmm.' Mike thinks for a few moments, sipping his wine.

'I wish you wouldn't make that slurping noise, Mike, it really gets on my nerves. Fiona Bruce wears well, don't you think? I wonder what facials she uses.'

'What does he do up in that room for so long?' Mike tilts his glass right back so the last of the wine slips onto his tongue.

'Oh Mike, for goodness sake, he's fourteen.'

'Aye, right.' He isn't satisfied with this as an explanation, but decides not to pursue it. He puts his arm around Beth and she automatically leans into him.

'It comes with being an only child,' she continues after a pause.

'What does?' Mike's mind is on other things.

'Being bright and deep. It's a shame we couldn't have had more.'

After years of trying and fertility treatment, they'd all but given up the idea of children, then along came Logan. It was like a miracle. The walls are hung with framed photographs of all the milestones of his fourteen years; the three of them on the day of his birth, his first day at school, receiving a medal at a swimming gala, astride a camel in Lanzarote. He can do no wrong and even now their hearts ache with pride in him.

'I just wish he had more friends,' Mike says after a while.

'We're very lucky. He doesn't drink or take drugs, and he's never in any bother.'

'Aye, I know, but he'd do well to go out more.'

'I know what you mean, Mike.' Beth presses her head further into his side. They'd had these conversations countless times before. They sit quietly till the news draws to a close. 'Remind me to Google about Fiona Bruce's facial before we go to bed, Mike.'

They always sit around the table for meals. One day, over tea, Logan speaks about his forthcoming birthday.

'I've been thinking about what I'd like for my present.'

'Oh aye, son?' They had always given him everything he wanted, within reason.

Logan's phone makes a noise and he steals a glimpse at the lit up screen under the table and grins.

'Anyone we know?' ventures his mother, looking across at him. He doesn't seem to get many calls and whilst she doesn't approve of phones at the table, she feels a little flutter of excitement on his behalf that someone is in touch with him.

'No. Just a friend'.

They eat in silence for a few moments.

'What were you saying son, about your birthday,' picks up Mike. He twirls some pasta round his fork and his white shirt becomes spattered with spots of tomato sauce.

'Oh, Mike, I told you you should have changed when you came in from work. Now I'll need to get the Vanish out.'

'It's fine.' He dabs at it with his hankie which he dampens with spit.

'Mike, please!' said Beth.

There is another silence. 'Well son?', asks Mike after a time.

'Naw, but you'll think it's weird.' He draws circles with his fork in the residue of red bolognaise sauce that is spread over his plate. He loves the way the little white channels filled up again after two seconds.

'Don't do that love, it's beginning to get on my nerves. Come on, though; tell us what you'd like, as long as it's not alive! We couldn't do with any more of those gerbils, could we, Mike?' She smiles at the impossibility of the idea.

Do they really think he is still at that stage? he wonders. His friends' parents all seem so cool compared to his. They sometimes seem to him as if they had been born in the wrong time or been beamed down from another world. 'I'd like a coffin for my birthday,' he says.

Beth and Mike, sitting side by side, opposite Logan, each have a forkful of pasta heading towards their mouths, and each pause and lowered their forks, like a little choreographed scene, which makes Logan smile, despite himself.

'A what?'

'What do you mean, love?'

They both look at him, in that concerned way they have, searching unbearably, so that he can feel tears of humiliation coming. He looks down at his plate and makes a last white spiral before putting down his fork with a clatter. 'A coffin. You know, a coffin, like they bury people in. I'd like a coffin for my birthday.'

There is a bit of a silence. Mike raises his fork again and it drips juice like blood from a cut.

'Bit of a strange idea, that, son. Are you joking with us?'

Logan blows his nose.

Beth pokes Mike in the ribs. 'Quiet, Mike. But what for love?' she asks, in that gentle tone she has that Logan finds increasingly annoying.

'I just want one, okay?'

They had all put their cutlery down, but now Mike resumes his chewing. It always gets on Logan's nerves, they way his dad parts his lips and sucks in the air as he eats, but he'll never tell him. He'll turn into him one day. His gran is always saying how like each other they look.

'Talk to us about it, love.'

'Please don't call me that, mum.'

'Sorry. I do try not to, but you know, it's hard to stop after all this time.'

There is another silence and Logan becomes aware of the thrum of the fridge and the gentle tick of the Ikea clock on the wall, its second hand twitching in a pointless round. Beth gives one of her helpful prompts. 'Logan, love? Sorry. Logan?'

He looks up at her, shakes his head, and says, 'Someone I was talking to told me their grandma slept with a coffin under her bed. It reminded her of her mortality. And that made her feel more alive. Life was sharper with more meaning. I don't know, I can't describe it properly. The world's such a mess. It's your generation, actually; burning down the rainforests, global warming, extinction of the rhinos. Trump!

Bolsanaro! He looks up at them, the last two words summarising everything, he thinks. He hopes they'll see how obvious it is, though he's frustrated that he can't express himself more clearly.

'Bolsanaro? Which team does he play for?' asks Mike.

Logan looks at the ceiling.

'We do our best, Logan', says Beth, looking hurt. 'I always get ethically sourced fish now, and we sponsored you on that Greenpeace walk you did.'

'Who was it you were talking to, son?' asks Mike.

'It doesn't matter. That's not the point.' He leans back in his chair and begins fingering his spots.

'Don't do that love, you'll make them worse. Did you put your cream on today?'

Logan rolls his eyes in an exaggerated gesture.

'Is your friend's grandma still alive?' Beth shoots Mike a knowing look, but his expression is blank.

Logan rocks back on his chair and shows them his palms in a gesture of surrender. 'Yes, I think so, I can't remember, it's not relevant.'

More mystery, thinks Beth. 'We'd been thinking of a new laptop,' she says, testing him.

Logan sighs. 'I've got my phone. I don't need a laptop.'

'I'm sorry, son, but I think a coffin's a bit morbid for a fifteenth birthday present; well, for any birthday present actually. In fact I think it's out of the question.' Mike is unusually assertive.

'I knew you'd say that. I'm off upstairs.' His chair drums on the laminate floor as he pushes it back to get up.

'No, wait love,' says Beth standing up too.

'Sit down, son. Come on let's talk about it.' But he has already left the room.

'Let him go Mike, let him go,' Beth says, in a tone which implies it is all his fault. 'I'll talk to him later.'

Later, Mike and Beth sit in bed, propped up on pillows, with open books, lying unread across their quilt-covered groins. 'I just can't get into this PD James,' says Mike.

'Oh, I quite liked that one. You need to work at things a bit more Mike, that's your problem. But I can't seem to concentrate myself tonight.'

'Do you think he needs counselling?'

'Oh come on, Mike. What were you like at fourteen?'

'Nearly fifteen. I liked girls and football. I was pretty straightforward, I think.' He shuffles about under the duvet, and the movement makes his book close, so he loses his place. 'Damn.' He flicks through the pages. 'Do you think he's... you know...'

'What?'

'Well I've wondered for a while if, maybe he's, you know, a bit gay?'

Beth removes her reading glasses and twists round to look at him. 'A *bit* gay? What do you mean, a *bit* gay?'

'Well, I suppose it's all a bit experimental at that age isn't it? Maybe he's not sure.'

'It doesn't matter, does it, as long as he's happy?'

'No, no, of course not.' But Mike would find it a disappointment, however much he tried to accept it.

She sucks at the arm of her glasses for a moment. 'Maybe it's just a whim. Maybe he'll forget.'

'About being gay?'

'No, Mike, for goodness sake, about the coffin.'

'Oh, aye.'

They put their books down on the bedside tables, turn off the lights and make love. It is Friday, after all. Their passion would have astonished and disgusted Logan, who is busy on his phone in his room across the hall, his music gently throbbing in the background.

Beth keeps thinking about the coffin. On Monday she watches Logan eat his cereal before he sets off for school. He's kept a low profile over the weekend. His spots look as bad as ever. She scans the vibrant bobbing heads of the dahlias through the kitchen window, but she doesn't really see them.

'You would tell us if there was anything wrong, wouldn't you love?'

Logan rolls his eyes at the word. 'Muumm.'

'Sorry, I keep forgetting; 'cause we do love you, you know. I know it's not a word we use, not *cool*, but we do. We both do.' She bends over his shoulder and gives him a kiss.

He pulls away, 'Muumm. Please, give it a rest.' He pops the last spoonful of Weetabix into his mouth.

She lifts up the jar of marmalade off the table, ready to put away. 'Where would you keep this coffin anyway?'

He looks up at her and can't repress a smile. 'Under my bed, of course. That's the idea. You sleep on top of it, so you're reminded that death's on the horizon somewhere, and it helps you focus on being alive.'

She thinks for moment. 'But you've got a high bed.'

'I've thought of that. I'd use it as a table, and I'd keep stuff in it. You're always saying we need more storage space.'

'Your dad's not keen. I'll have to talk to him.' She picks up the cereal packet and tucks it under her arm so she can manage the used mugs as well.

'Thanks Mum.' He kisses her on her cheek for the first time in weeks, and heads off for school. There is a bounce in his step. Beth smiles to herself as she watches him go. There is no denying he is a fine boy.

'Where d'you go to buy a coffin, anyway?' Mike asks Logan a couple of days later. 'And what would the neighbours think when they saw it coming into the house?'

'I've searched the net. You can order by email and they get delivered in a flat-pack.'

'Well I suppose it would be good experience, putting it together,' says Beth. 'At parents' night Mr Brown said architecture might be something to consider when the time comes to go to Uni.'

Mike looks at her, but says nothing.

So they order the coffin: *a unique Scandinavian design, made from eco-friendly wood,* and sure enough it comes in a flat-pack, so that none of the neighbours know; it would have been difficult to explain. Beth and Mike had always wrapped Logan's birthday presents up, and Beth insists they gift-wrap the coffin, even though Logan has seen it in the corner of the garage. She finds a leftover roll of Celtic football club wallpaper, though Logan has drifted away from that particular beautiful game over the last year, and at breakfast on the big day they present him with the package, as if it were a surprise. He is all smiles, and later, when he gets home from school he goes straight up to his room and begins assembling it with an allen key, just like an Ikea kit, the diagrammatic instructions laid out on the floor. He comes down for tea, high and happy.

'How's it going, love?'

'Fine,' he says, not even noticing Beth's epithet, which normally makes him snap or scowl.

'Can we come and see it?'

'You'll have to wait till it's finished.'

'Do you want a hand, son? I used to be quite good at woodwork.' Mike has a mouthful of fish pie and talks through his chewing, but Logan doesn't seem to notice.

'Come off it Dad, remember the shelves you tried to put up? The whole wall had to be re-plastered.' Logan laughs at the memory and Beth joins in.

'Okay, but the walls in these new houses are so thin,' says Mike, happy to be the cause of mirth. 'Just plaster board. Not easy you know?'

'No, I want this to last, Dad. I probably won't need it for years. Decades. A lifetime, you know?'

They brighten further at this thought, and he leaves the table to get back to his carpentry by numbers.

'He seems really excited,' says Beth.

It is late before Logan finishes putting the coffin together. Beth and Mike are invited upstairs to have a look. It is resting on two stools under the high-rise bed. It has a mahogany veneer and plastic brass-effect handles. The lid is hinged in two sections. Logan opens the top section up, where one day his lifeless head will rest. There are piles of neatly folded T-shirts, resting against the purple satin quilt lining. 'See all the storage?'

'Well, I must say, I think it's quite nice,' says Beth, running her fingers against the silky surface of the veneer. 'What do you think, Mike?'

'Aye, you've done a good job there, son.' Then he sees the brass plate on the lid, with a blue-tacked piece of paper on the top, saying "Logan Lynch" and giving his date of birth, followed by a dash. 'I don't know about that though, son. I think that's going a bit too far.'

'But that 's the whole point of it Dad,' says Logan in an exasperated tone. 'It has to be *your* coffin. *My* coffin, you know? So that you know it's for you, and it will keep you grounded to the earth; to life.'

Logan is chatty all week, and on the Friday evening there is a knock at the door. When Beth opens it there are two girls and a boy on the step, asking for Logan.

Beth eyes them with a mixture of surprise and joy, and calls up the stairs to him.

His head appears over the banister at the top and he shouts down, 'Oh hi. Just come on up.'

'Are you sure, love?'

'Yea, what's the problem, Mum?'

'Oh nothing, I suppose.' She smiles at the three visitors as they take their shoes off. 'I'm Logan's mum,' she says. They don't introduce themselves, but smile back to her, used to having to humour parents, and go upstairs. Beth is impressed that they have removed their shoes. They must be okay. She and Mike can hear and feel the beat of metal music a short time afterwards.

'Was that a girl?' asked Mike.

'Two actually.' They exchange knowing looks, and smile. 'Come on Mike; let's finish the washing up.'

Up in the bedroom, Logan's friends are admiring his coffin. 'Cool,' one of them says, adding, 'My parents would never let me have one of these. You're so lucky, man.' The music of Rage Against the Machine fills the air. You can't beat the old classics. Logan's head nods to the beat.

The coffin comes to be accepted by Beth as another piece of furniture that she dusts each Tuesday. It comes up really nicely with a squirt of Pledge.

Their wedding anniversary is coming up. 'Let's do something special,' suggests Mike, pausing in his labours over PD James one night. 'It's twenty-five years after all.'

'Yes, I've been thinking,' said Beth. She switches off her bedside light and lies on her side facing him.

'What?' he asks, curious about her mysterious tone. He switches off his own lamp and shuffles towards her.

'No, you'll think I'm daft.' She snuggles up to him and he pushes his nose into her ear, even though it isn't Friday.

'No, go on, love.'

His hand feels its way up and down her thigh. She interlaces her fingers with his. 'I think we should buy a couple of coffins, for under the bed.' Mike withdraws his nose and stops stroking her soft, smooth flesh. But just for a second.

'Sounds like a plan,' he says, and their lips become locked together.

4

Silver for Good luck

'I don't want to see it', she had said, her voice empty and cold. 'Take it away.' This after six hours of labour when she had been at their mercy, and they had seen her, naked and raw and in agony, the tattooed butterfly on her shoulder quivering in her sweat. There had been no small-talk in the intervals between her contractions, just monosyllables and silence; she had made her feelings clear when she was admitted. It was a concealed pregnancy; concealed until the onset of labour, when she allowed a neighbour to seek help. Concealed in a way, and yet expected too, but something which couldn't be thought about till it had to be. The birth was straightforward; this thing had to be ejected from her body, and she had to get back to her child as quickly as possible. The child at home: *her* child, not this baby. This couldn't be hers, it just wasn't possible. They had talked gently with her, but it was no use; she wouldn't see the baby, would not give him a name. 'Take it away,' she had said, so icily and finally that everyone knew there was no arguing with her. He had been expunged from her life. She hadn't even stayed in the hospital overnight; she'd just collected her few things together and had left without asking about him, or leaving any trace of herself behind.

The baby lies in a clear plastic cot, clothed in a used babygro and wrapped in hospital blankets. It. The baby. He. He exudes the smell of the newness of life. Sometimes he cries, like a lost baby animal of some sort, like a wild kitten from a remote hill-farm, but he has no voice. The world is incredibly bright. The world is the office. The hospital no longer has a nursery for the newborn babies; they stay next to their mothers until they are discharged, sometimes just after a few hours, to an idea of homeliness; happy parents and welcoming brothers and sisters perhaps, in warm cosy rooms where everyone wears slippers. But there is no mother, so there is nowhere to put the baby except the office. The office is full of white light from the fluorescent tubes and from the sun, which streams in through the large windows and from the adjacent rooms separated by glass partitions; all part of ward nine, the maternity ward.

There is a constant traffic of people through the office. Nurses and doctors complete their paperwork, and collect surgical paraphernalia. They come and go, stepping around the baby, whose cot is conveniently on wheels so can be glided aside to allow easier access to cupboards. Somehow in all this confusion of staff about their business a succession of people know to check on the baby. His temperature is taken regularly and his nappy is changed. He is given milk through a latex nipple by a nurse on shift, and when cradled frowns and screws up his eyes against the brightness, giving himself a wise look, though he can't know anything. There is a problem with his stomach, which is inflamed for some reason. He cries a lot and seems to be in pain.

The nurses write their notes. They wear white cotton uniforms, which are dazzling in the light. It is very warm unless you sit still. The babies need the warmth. The nurses chat between their chores.

'I told you Dave had shaved his beard off, didn't I?'

'You did. I can't wait to see him.'

'You'll have to be quick: he's growing it again.'

'Why's that then? I thought you said everyone said it made him look years younger.'

'Aye, it does. He says everyone'd expect more of him. So he's growing it again.'

They both laugh, then carry on with their notes.

The miracle of birth: the first birthday, when you're nothing. Will he remember anything? Was it dark inside the womb, or was he enfolded by a secure red blanket of translucent flesh, like the hand-drawn pictures in handbooks written for prospective parents, with the baby curled up inside, soothed by the sound of the double-beat of his mother's heart, and the surge of blood around her body. The blood which had nurtured him during the nine months it had taken for him to change from speck to tadpole to boy.

The door to the office is left open, and squeaky footsteps sound regularly down the endless corridor. It is a busy place; a surreal door to the world for the baby, but not for those who come and go. Full of hospital smells that stay in the memory forever. Will he remember any of this? A feeling of deja vu in middle-age perhaps, without knowing the connections? Or as a toddler in a foetal position, sucking his thumb while in bed with a sore tummy, and holding a piece of bedding to his nose for comfort? It is very warm in the room, but his temperature is below normal. He has had no contact with the warm skin of his mother, nor been coaxed to suck her nourishing milk or be moistened by the brush of her kiss.

Enfolded by blankets in his plastic cot he cries with eyes tight shut. Two women enter and there is discussion with a nurse. They have come for the baby: a social worker and a foster carer. The office is not comfortable for visitors: they are sweating from their climb up the stairs into the heat, and there is nowhere to sit. They are intruders with the potential to create disorder within the machinery of the institution, though no-one asks for their ID. The social worker introduces herself and the carer.

'We're here for the baby. I phoned earlier.' She's young and is slightly flustered; it feels a big responsibility and the hospital is disempowering. It takes a while to find someone who understands all the threads and can draw them together, but eventually a sister appears.

'I tried to phone you, but you'd left. He's got a problem with his tummy and we're not sure you can take him today. The doctor needs to see him to decide, but she's in theatre just now.'

The sister and the social worker take each other in; they've both got their jobs to do and they each have their own ideas. The foster carer has gone over to the plastic cot. 'Is this him? Poor wee mite. Hello there, hello little feller.' She puts her index finger inside his curled up hand and he grasps it in a tiny fist. Those who are in the room stop what they are doing and look on.

'It's an awful business,' the sister says, 'not to be wanted like that. Poor little scrap. You wonder what's in his mother's mind.' She holds her head slightly to one side, watching the foster mother bending over the cot. 'We get them now and again. A couple of weeks ago we had a fifteen year old in who'd had her baby in the toilet; right in the bowl at home, and her parents didn't even know she was pregnant. That one turned out all right, depending on how you look at it. The girl's parents took them both home; they seemed thrilled to bits in a funny kind of way.' She's a professional, and stays detached. She looks back at her notes. The baby starts crying so the foster mother picks him up, without asking. She rocks him in experienced arms that have comforted dozens of babies over the years: she can't be much under sixty, and soon he stops crying and looks around through blue unfocussed eyes. She talks away to him as they shuffle around the room together in a tragi-comic waltz that makes the others smile. He seems to look outside. The sky is icy blue, and there is nothing in it for the eye to focus on but endless space; a line of nothingness till crossed by an unseen star. Then, from somewhere, a crying gull wheels and circles on its sharp-eyed hunt for discarded scraps, a blood-red drop painted on its screaming beak.

The social worker has produced a camera from her handbag. 'Do you mind if we take some pictures? He'll need something as he grows up. I don't suppose the midwife who delivered him is around?' She isn't of course. But a registrar and a couple of nurses are persuaded to stand beside the foster carer and the baby for some pictures. He's stopped crying and they all smile at the camera. He's the focus of everyone's attention now: those who come and go on various errands through the office pause to take in the tableau. What will they tell him when he's older? How will they explain to him that his mother wouldn't look at him or hold him, and didn't give him a name, or will they make up a different story? What story will go with the photographs when they are creased and dog-eared with much handling? Or will it all be kept a secret?

He's a bit of a curiosity in the office. 'He's the baby the mother couldn't even name. It's so sad, isn't it? I could just take him home with me. What will happen to the little one now?'

The social worker and the sister chat away. 'We'll take it slowly. We know where his mother lives. She'll need time to think things through. We'll see if we can get her some counselling; help her look at the options and hear about the supports which are available. At the end of the day he might go for adoption: there's plenty families waiting for babies.' It's wearisome work; she's seen so many children go home and have to come back into care again and again, until they reach the point that they're so difficult that no-one wants to adopt them. She takes out some paperwork from her briefcase and writes something down.

*

The girl sits in her fourth floor fat in a high-rise across town. The mother. She is just eighteen years old. She looks across the room to the door, which has been smashed in several times. Brown sticky tape binds a series of crazy cracks in a frosted glass panel to the side.

Finn has been out since morning; he needs to score and she doesn't know when he'll be back. She lights a cigarette and looks at her child playing with some mashed up food in a dish on the floor. A thin mongrel pads about. 'Go and lie down,' she shouts and she raises her hand in an angry gesture as it slinks off to its bed in the corner. The flat was in a mess when she got home from the hospital, with dirty dishes left on chairs, and clothes lying all over the place. The television has gone; Finn's sold it, but won't admit the fact. She knows. The child holds out a fist full of mashed up food for her to take, but she looks away. She tries not to let herself think about the baby, but a desperate sob keeps forcing itself into her throat. She fingers a row of gold studs which follow the curve of her ear. It will be better this way; she just wouldn't have been able to cope. She keeps thinking of her own mother and of the years she spent in foster care and children's homes, waiting to return to the idea of the mother she loved, but finding instead a woman who wanted only her money from the social and her help, but could give nothing in return.

There are three gentle knocks at the door. She just sits there suppressing her sobs.

*

The baby seems to have fallen asleep, so the foster carer lies him gently in the cot and tucks the blanket around him. 'Doctor's still in theatre I'm afraid,' says the sister coming back into the office after checking the progress of a woman in labour in one of the birthing rooms. 'I'm afraid she could be ages yet. If she's not happy about his tummy he'll need to stay in.' It's plain that she wants them to leave.

'We'll stay a bit and see, eh?' The foster mother wants to take the baby away from all this. The social worker smiles in acquiescence, giving in to the foster mother's matriarchal assertiveness, but she knows they're not wanted. She glances at her watch; she has visits to make, and has tickets for the theatre in the evening. They decide to go and have a cup of tea at the Red Cross cafe and come back later.

While they are away the doctor calls in and says the baby will need to be monitored for another night. When they return the social worker arranges to telephone in the morning, and if all is well they will collect the baby then. The foster mother is reluctant to leave. She strokes the baby's cheek and puts some silver next to his pillow: a fifty pence piece and some loose change; a gift of good luck where she comes from. 'We'll see you tomorrow little feller, don't you fret.' They walk off slowly down the corridor, their shoes squealing like the other footsteps on the shiny, highly polished floor. Later on a nurse feeds the baby and finds the money. It puzzles her for a moment, but she puts it on the reception desk and it's soon forgotten.

There are six new births on the ward during the course of the following night. The cries of mothers and their new babies echo around the corridor from time to time. For a while the office is empty except for the baby. He stirs in the plastic hospital cot, listening to the sounds, his wrinkled face twisting from side to side as, whimpering, he searches for the comfort of his mother's breast. Somewhere in the other world beyond the office a whale will be singing in secret green depths and a wolf will be howling to a crescent moon.

The next morning Sister wonders who has left the money on her desk. She counts it out. Eighty-five pence. An odd amount and she can't account for it. It annoys her. She asks around but no-one knows anything about it. It is difficult to keep track of everything when people come and go on their shifts all the time. She looks in the main office. The abandoned baby is still there. She takes her turn at holding it. Poor little mite. They hope it will be able to go to the foster carer later in the day. She goes back to her place at the reception desk to answer a call. Absently she puts the silver into a Sick Kids collecting tin that stands on the edge.

5

Spaghetti Junction

'What's in the bag?' asks Nathan. He's bouncing down the stairs in his Save Our Seas T-shirt as Alison comes in through the front door.

'Never you mind. It's a surprise. You'll have to wait.' She pulls the bag close to her as Nathan reaches out towards it.

'You can't do that. That's shan!'

Alison finds it hard to keep up with the way young people invent new words and change the meanings of old ones. It's like a different language intended to maintain adults at arm's length, with constantly shifting rules so they won't be able to keep up.

It's a John Lewis carrier bag, and the corners of a box inside distort the shining plastic, tantalisingly inviting curiosity. Nathan tilts his head, trying to make out the shadow-like lettering, which just shows through as Alison, arms stretched with the weight of shopping, passes him in the hall, but she twirls away, thwarting him. 'Later,' she says smiling, delighted at his interest.

'Awe, Alison.' He heads off to the lounge. Alison watches him go. She adores that curly hair of his. No doubt, like his brother he'll want it all shaved off in his teens. She sighs.

They all call her Alison, except Peter who nearly always calls her Mum. She and Peter have been married for twenty years now. Manacled together, he says, quoting Basil Fawlty. It would be funnier if he didn't say it so often. 'Anyone seen Mum?' Peter will ask, even when he doesn't need her for anything. He seems to need to know where she is, just in case. Alison wonders how he'd manage if she went first. Died that is. Best to go together, he says. Depends when, she says. And they all call him Peter, including Alison, except when she calls him Darling. She calls all of them Darling a lot of the time, and it makes them cringe when their pals come round. It started off as a joke, Peter and Alison mimicking Brian and Jennifer from the Archers, but now she just can't stop.

Alison sets down the bags of supermarket shopping in the chaotic kitchen, the disorder an inevitable consequence of busy lives and three growing children, and heads up the creaking stairs of the old Victorian semi clutching her John Lewis bag. She meets Dylan at the turn. 'John Lewis?' he enquires, with a slight turn of his upper lip below the darkening shadow which he's been trying to cultivate by unnecessary shaving. 'Makes a change from the charity shops. Not somebody's birthday is it?' He glances between her and the screen of his phone, revealing a trace of a tattoo as he bends; the cause of much weeping on the part of Alison when he came home with it earlier in the year.

When the kids were younger, they were part of her. As babies they hid their faces in her breasts and clung to her as if she was everything. And through the toddler years they came to her with uninhibited love, and she kissed their naked tummies and breathed in the scent of innocent purity they exuded. They saw her as an extension of themselves, taking her totally for granted, and she loved it. Now they are pulling away into their own worlds just as the universe expands at an ever quickening rate, and she feels she knows them less and less, even Nathan, who she still thinks of as the baby. At times they feel like strangers. But that's our job, isn't it? Peter had told her, to make them independent, so they can make their own way in the world. But that couldn't be right. Surely they could still be friends? Alison had said. Peter seems content to just let them go. He is already looking forward to holidays with just the two of them and to more order and quiet.

She reaches up to lift Dylan's fringe, but he pulls his head out of the way. She catches a whiff of Lynx. 'Are you out tonight?' she asks.

'Dunno', he says, continuing down the stairs, his eyes on his phone.

She asks herself if his pupils are dilated, if he might be on something. But she'd only seen into his eyes briefly. Those beautiful brown eyes. She wonders if she should do a furtive search of his room when he goes out, but she still hasn't recovered from the last time, when she found the porn magazines. Normal at his age, Peter had said when she'd shared her horror with him, but she shudders at the memory. Her little boy.

'You'll fall,' she says, but he's gone, so sure of himself and where he's going in life that he doesn't need to look. She's so proud of what he's become, but at the same time aching for the loss of the child that he no longer is. It's sometimes hard to believe he's hers; that they're all hers.

Alison hides the bag in her wardrobe beneath the rail of her clothes that hang there like the sloughed skins of somebody else. She almost hopes that one of them will want to sneak a look. They know that she always hides the Christmas presents there. She looks at herself in the mirrored wardrobe door as she closes it, singing quietly. "Who knows where the time goes..." She takes off the clothes she wears to work and puts on an Indian print skirt. "Across the evening sky, all the birds are leaving..."

Back on the landing Alison pauses outside Kate's door: 'Hello, Darling,' she calls, tapping gently with her knuckles, a bit like the clocking of the death watch beetle that she fears has invaded the crumbling old house. She's mentioned it to Peter, but he doesn't seem concerned. 'Turn it down a bit will you?' At first there's no reply, and the band, Prodigy, doesn't waver in its modulations. Alison opens the door and puts her head around the corner. 'Kate, darling...'

'Yes, okay, Alison,' Kate replies, in an exasperated tone that suggests that Alison is asking something very unreasonable.

'How was your day, darling?'

'Yea, okay, the usual, you know.'

'Your room could do with a bit of a clean and tidy, Kate, couldn't it?'

'It's not that bad. And I've got this essay to write, you know.'

'We could maybe do it together?'

'How familiar are you with King Lear?'

'The room, Kate darling.'

'Nah, don't worry. I've got a system.'

Alison leaves it there. Kate's nose piercing glints in the lamplight. At least for now they've dissuaded her from getting her tongue pierced. Still glowing at the prospect of her surprise for all of them, Alison goes back downstairs to make the supper. The evening meal had always been called supper in her childhood; taken with napkins and good table manners, and she persists in calling it supper, even though the associated image of cosy fires, carpet slippers and togetherness isn't reflected in her current family experience. By now the boys are in the living room. Nathan is watching a film on his tablet in which a great white shark emerges from the depths to rip apart young nubiles in foaming sea the colour of ketchup, and Dylan is scrolling and chuckling to himself. Nathan hasn't got his earphones on and the bass strings accompanying the briny slaughter on the tablet keep intruding. 'Keep it down, Nathan, will you?' But Nathan just keeps on munching his Doritos impassively. It could get physical later, but they are guaranteed soft landings; there are piles of clean but crumpled laundry on the armchairs and on the floor; they never seem to get to the final stage of being ironed and folded away in drawers. The heaps of washing just shift about, collapsing and being hastily re-built during the early morning panic to find clean pants, T-shirts or unmatchable socks. The boys seem to prefer odd socks, choosing garish colour-combinations to provoke, but Peter just gets weary with the search; he wears the same pair till they go stiff, and is always secretly buying new ones, which of course adds to the problem of lonely, singleton socks. He's in the other front room just now, in his wing-backed chair, with classical music from Spotify nourishing his brain and a glass of whisky in his hand. He's recovering from another day spent in front of rows of sullen teenagers not wanting to learn history. It's the room where, in theory, he and Alison entertain guests; relatively tidy but undusted. There's never the time to get on top of things.

After a while Alison gets busy in the kitchen and there's a familiar sound of the clash of steel saucepans, the rush of running water and the banging of cupboard doors. On the radio Evan Davis keeps interrupting an exasperated politician trying to explain the Government's policy on public transport. 'Sounds like pasta again,' mutters Dylan to no-one in particular. He quietly sings a parody of a John Lennon song: 'Imagine there's no pasta, it's easy if you try.'

After a while Alison goes in to the hall and calls out in a sing-songy, homely voice that supper's ready. She repeats it a few minutes later and then again after that. At last doors can be heard opening as Dylan and Nathan pause in their vicarious pursuits of death and social connections among the crumpled linen, and footfalls can be heard on the floor above.

'Yummy; pasta,' says Dylan, entering the kitchen first. 'That makes a nice change.' But everyone's become immune to his sarcasm.

'I thought we'd all eat together tonight, round the table,' says Alison. Dylan looks stunned. He notices the tablecloth, and the cutlery, all properly laid out around the rarely-used place-mats that have pictures of soft-focussed engravings of scenes from the Highlands. There are even paper serviettes, left over from the last time Peter's parents came for lunch a few weeks back. A large bowl of spaghetti steams at one end of the table and Alison is busy transferring the sauce to a serving dish beside the cooker. Her glasses have steamed up in the process and everything is a blur. Kate comes in, ready to do a smash and grab and get back to her rock music upstairs, but Alison plants herself in the doorway, the dish of sauce in her hands, and tells her that they're having a family meal tonight, Darling, and Kate sits, nonplussed.

Nathan comes into the kitchen. 'What for?' he asks, when Alison tells him the plan. She just smiles, but he persists. 'C'mon. That's pure shite. I'm in the middle of watching a film. I never get to do what I want to do,' and so on. Alison picks him up on his crude use of the English language and he subsides grumpily onto a chair as Peter sidles in, his earphones in place like a drip-feed to his head, the little white leads stretching to the iPod in his pocket. He doesn't seem to notice the groaning supper table, and automatically loads up his plate and begins to shuffle off, until Alison cuts him off at the threshold and shepherds him back to the table. With a tweak of her wrist, she takes his iPod from him and tells him he's got to eat with the rest of the family.

'Welcome to Spaghetti Junction, Peter,' says Dylan, as Alison gently pushes him down into a chair.

'What's all this about?' Kate asks. 'Is it somebody's birthday?'

'Why do you all think we have to wait until it's somebody's birthday before we can share a meal together?' says Alison. 'No,' she continues, 'I've been thinking...' She's standing at the head of the table, ladle raised, dripping bolognaise sauce onto the clean, unironed table-cloth, embroidered by her grandmother and handed down. Her eyes become moist, and the family sits awkwardly, till after a while Nathan hands her a serviette: 'Here Mum,' he says.

She's moved that he calls her mum and tears spring forth. 'Thanks, darling, I'm fine.' She blows her nose. 'Jane, you know my friend who's a social worker, told me about such a sad little boy she'd been working with; awful family background, you wouldn't believe it, and it just got me thinking about how lucky we are. So I just wanted us to celebrate that. We seem to be drifting apart at the moment and, I think we all need to be more...evolved.' She looks around at them all. Peter nods, but it's unclear if he's humouring her or agreeing with her. 'So, I thought we'd all have some Quality Time together tonight,' she says, beginning to hand round steaming plates to the perplexed upturned faces.

'Has anyone got a bucket handy?' hisses Dylan to Kate, 'I think I'm going to puke.' Kate frowns at him and digs him in the ribs.

'What's that darling?'

'I was just saying, lovely spaghetti, Alison.'

Alison smiles. She sweeps her hair behind her ears and sits down and soon there is the gentle clattering of cutlery on crockery and the soft churning of mastication.

After a while Alison says, 'Do you know what I heard the other day?' The clattering stops abruptly and everyone stops slurping for a moment. They all look at her as she dishes out sauce for herself, lastly. 'Apparently in eighty-five per cent of families everyone eats in their own room, or at different times with a screen of some sort in front of them. At least I think it was eighty-five per cent...' She reaches for the grated cheese, but the others have taken it all, so she puts the empty bowl back down, apparently unsurprised. '...Anyway it's some ridiculous number. And only one family in six eats together around the table. Something like that anyway. And then I heard about that little boy I was telling you about. The point is that family life is dying, apparently, and it all just makes me very sad.' Her eyes were glistening with moisture again. They are all desperate for her not to cry; she's been doing it quite a lot lately. 'I mean, not that *we* are like that. *We* are still a proper family. Look at us eating together tonight for example. But I think we need to come together a bit more, be a bit more *evolved*, what do you think?' Dylan is looking at his phone under the table and quietly puts it in his pocket at this point.

'Evolved?' Queries Nathan. 'Like the way we're related to apes and gorillas and stuff?'

'You know what Alison means,' rebukes Kate.

'I know you all think I'm daft, but that's the way I feel.' She stares absently at her grandmother's intricate needlepoint, now spattered with indelible sauce.

Nathan sucks in another worm of spaghetti. 'So I thought we'd all have a nice family game after supper, like we used to when you were little. Do you remember?'

At that moment Dylan chokes on a bay-leaf and has to get up and dash to the sink for a glass of water. They haven't played games together as a family for ages, not since the time they learned knock-out-whist from Peter when their flight was delayed on their way back from holiday a couple of year back and they had time to kill at the airport.

'What kind of game?' asks Kate.

'You'll have to wait and see,' says Alison. 'Nathan, have some salad, darling.' She holds out the wooden salad bowl towards him.

It falls quiet again, except for five pummelling mouths churning up Alison's culinary creation like a bank of washing machines in a launderette. After a while Alison attempts to get a conversation going. 'So what have you been up to today, Nathan?'

'Nothing.' Then with pushing; 'Just some stuff.' Then, 'Can I have a pet?'

As a family they hadn't had a lot of success with pets. There is Mrs Nesbitt, of course, who still has years ahead of her, scratching the furniture and bringing half dead feathery offerings through the cat-flap, and who is generally aloof, as if embarrassed by them all. The children don't see her as a proper pet; she's just part of the household. The real pets had all come to sticky ends. The budgie, Yorik, had got out of an open window and become the lunch of a passing sparrowhawk; Dmitri the Russian Dwarf hamster had bitten Kate the first time she handled it after it was brought home from Petula's Pets, and it had consequently spent a miserable but mercifully short life confined to his cage and sadly neglected; and Gerald the Gerbil was last seen alive in the jaws of Mrs Nesbitt, his wriggling tail dangling from her smiling mouth, in the living room window as the family drove away from the house to catch a plane to a resort in Crete. Dylan had been inconsolable, but they couldn't miss the plane.

'I don't know Nathan. What were you thinking of?

'A corn snake. I had a hold of Zeb's today and it's really cool.

'Oh, I'm not sure,' says Alison.

Nathan protests that everyone else had had a pet and why couldn't he, and life was unfair and he'd look after it and all they ate was frozen dead mice and what's the problem? Alison tells him that they'll see, and moves the conversation on to Kate, who tells of a girl in third year who is pregnant and has had to go into care. This isn't what Alison's looking for so she turns to Dylan who tells her that he and his friend, Chris, are thinking of going to a rock festival down south and wonders if they can borrow the old tent that no-one ever uses that's up in the attic somewhere.

'Oh, I'm not sure about a rock concert, darling, you hear of such awful stories...'

'What stories?' asks Dylan, genuinely not sure what she can mean.

'You know all that drug-taking and so on. What do you think Peter?'

'I don't know. We used to go to music festivals, remember?'

'Yes, I suppose, but it was different then, wasn't it?' Alison smiles in a kind of languid way and reaches across the corner of the table and takes Peter's hand. The spaghetti he has laboriously coiled up using the bowl of his spoon unravels as he has to let go of the fork he's holding. 'Oh, Peter, darling. We had some good times, didn't we.'

Peter tries to remember and uses his free hand to drain the tumbler of whisky he managed to retrieve from the front room earlier. 'The best is yet to come,' he says. She smiles, gets up and gives him a kiss on his cheek from behind. Dylan looks at them from across the table and vows to himself never to get married.

After supper Alison clears the table while the rest of the family sits there, waiting. 'Don't any of you move,' she warns. There's an understanding that she needs to be humoured, which even Nathan seems to share. Dylan looks restlessly at the time on his phone and rolls his eyes at Peter, who frowns at him.

They help her stack the dishes by the sink. She leaves the room for a few moments and they hear her go upstairs. The low rumble of their conversation subsides as she comes back with her parcel. Feelings of shock, disappointment and incredulity stir within them as from inside the John Lewis carrier bag she pulls a box of ... Monopoly. 'There,' she says, and the mid-life lines on her face radiate outwards in triumphant pleasure.

'Are you sure this is ideologically sound,' asks Dylan. 'What about all that stuff you go on about; you know, the evils of capitalism and all that?'

'It's just a harmless game,' she says. 'Something to bring us together. I used to love Monopoly as a child. We had a set when you were all younger, do you remember? I don't know what became of it.' The rest of the family look at each other, wondering which of them could have done away with the Monopoly. It's like a game of Cluedo in itself, thinks Dylan. He suspects Mr Happy over there with the matches in the garden incinerator. Peter avoids his gaze, but then he often does.

Alison unfolds the board and begins to arrange the cards and money, all of which has to be cut free from little polythene bags. 'The little houses used to be made of wood when I was little,' she sighs. Peter claims not to understand the rules. 'Maybe I should sit this one out,' he says. 'I could do the dishes.'

'No, no,' says Alison, 'I'm sure you'll get the hang of it,' and she begins reading rapidly from the booklet of rules, muttering hurriedly so the whole thing sounds unintelligible. Peter sighs. Kate takes over: she's into maths, facts and order. 'You each get fifteen hundred pounds at the start,' she says, and the one who shakes the highest goes first. And you can buy any unsold property you land on and trade with the other players to get sets. I remember it all now. You can't buy houses unless you've got a set.'

'I don't know what we'd do without you Kate,' says, Dylan, 'but we'd be bloody happy,' he adds in a stage whisper. She sticks her tongue out at him.

The rules of the game come back to them quickly, except for Peter, who claims not to understand, and demonstrates remarkable ineptitude: he's the old boot, but when it's his go he keeps driving Nathan's car, sometimes in the wrong direction.

Monopoly can be a long game. At first, with the possible exception of Peter, they all seem to be quite enjoying it, despite their protests at the start. But after an hour there's still a pile of unsold properties, and boredom has driven Nathan to trace his initials on the underside of the table with the edge of a spoon. Peter has managed to buy only the Old Kent Road, and is on the slippery slide to bankruptcy. He keeps forgetting to collect his two hundred pounds each time he passes Go, and seems to land repeatedly on squares with demands for income tax, or to pick up the Community Chest cards with bills for school fees or birthday presents.

The rest of the family have acquired fairly even piles of real estate and have begun to test the water for swaps. Alison persuades Kate to exchange Oxford Street for a couple of stations, and soon has first houses, then hotels, and everybody is mortgaging property to pay her rent, or taking refuge in jail.

'It says here you can still collect rents while you're in Jail,' Kate tells Nathan, waving the rules leaflet at him and demanding sixteen pounds he owes in rent. 'So there. Tidy!'

'That's crap. You can't do that.'

Soon Peter's in jail, everything he's got is mortgaged, he can't throw a double and he's out. Alison takes the whole thing very seriously and insists his property is taken over by the bank, though she can't find a reference in the rules to this eventuality. Alison is the banker. Peter slopes off, quietly, and as he leaves Dylan sees just the ghost of a smile as he switches on his iPOD and adjusts his earphones.

As the game of Monopoly proceeds, Nathan follows a policy of not buying houses or bartering with the others to try and get complete sets of property. When challenged he says he just likes the cash. It's a doomed strategy, of course, and before long his failure as a capitalist is sealed and he's returned to the vicarious delights of slaughter among the fishes in the living room. Kate and Dylan slog it out in classic sibling rivalry, but as always in Monopoly, when things begin to tilt in a certain way there's an inevitability about the outcome, and soon Dylan concedes, leaving Kate and Alison to hungrily pick over the entrails of his property deeds. He goes to his room, and after a time Kate too is insolvent and heads upstairs where the distant thump of The Chemical Brothers starts up. Quality Time is over. Alison loads the dishwasher and puts the kettle on for some coffee. After a while she goes into the hall. 'Would anyone like another game?' she calls. There's no response.

Later on, Dylan finishes another computer game and decides to head out to meet someone. Before leaving he goes into the kitchen to find a snack. Alison's still there. She's sitting at the table talking to herself. There's a nearly empty bottle of Rioja on the table and she's just draining a glass. A cigarette is balanced between two fingers, its blue smoke curling up to merge with the fog that hangs in the air. Dylan has never seen her smoke. The Monopoly board is set out again and she's shaking the dice. There's a hollow clatter as the dice tumble over the board. 'Sheven,' she says, and she moves the battleship, 'One, two, three, four, five, shix... sheven. Oh, Coventry Street. Yesh, I think I'll buy that.' She fumbles about with a bundle of fake money, which ends up all over the floor. 'Bollocks,' she says, but she completes the transaction, handing over the cash to the bank (she's the bank) and giving herself the change. 'Right, thatsh grrreat.' She giggles and gets up, moving round the table to the next chair, shakes the dice again and this time moves the Scotty dog and lands on the Chance square. 'Go to Jail, move directly to Jail, do not pash Go and do not collect two hundred pounds.' She stresses the word "not". 'Bastards. Never mind, I can shtill collect my rentsh, so sod the lot of you.' She moves on to the next chair and in the process a large fart escapes from her. 'Oops,' she says. 'What would Mother say? Funny bottom noise!' She giggles again and shakes the dice.

Dylan looks on open mouthed for a few moments, then reverses quietly out of the kitchen.

6

The Light of the World

The boy sits in the sofa, hungrily eating his poke of chips with his fingers. They're soaked in sauce and covered in salt, just the way he likes them. It's a brown velvet sofa, old now, abused and collapsed inside itself, so that despite the boy's small size his knees come up and he's bent in the middle. In the sofa, not on it. Not too good for the digestion. He shuffles around a bit; he couldn't find any underpants in the morning and he's uncomfortable. His clothes are a couple of sizes too big. Mick sits looking at him, drooling. He's wearing his most endearing face, with ears pricked and sad appealing eyes. His tail twitches, and the boy throws him a chip. The dog swallows it in a single gulp, licks his whiskers then edges a bit closer. The telly is on; like a beacon it pulls the boy into the semi-safety of its comforting world, so that the things happening in the house are like images flickering on the margins. His father's in the hall, doing "business" with a client. He likes to call them clients. The boy hasn't seen the client, but periodically the raised voices make it difficult for him to hear the television. But no-one will mess with his dad: word has got around that he has a gun. Not that anyone has seen it yet, but who would want to call him a liar?

The boy's sister comes into the room from a door that connects to one of the bedrooms adjoining. 'Mam wants to see you,' she says, and she throws herself down in the sofa, at the opposite end. She doesn't try to catch his eye, and immediately succumbs to the seduction of the telly, watching it through the lank streaks of her hair that hang down over her eyes. The boy carries on eating his chips as if he hasn't heard. They sit in a kind of torpor for several minutes, the sounds of the argument in the hall rising and falling in waves, so that sometimes the swearing can be distinctly heard before subsiding back to quieter tones of negotiation.

There's an old blanket nailed up at the window to stop the sunlight competing with the pictures on the T.V. screen. One of the walls is painted a patchy green, in contrast to the ancient flocked wallpaper of the others; an attempt by dad to brighten the place up a couple of years ago. There's a smell of urine and greasy food behind an odour of clinging cigarette smoke; all sealed within the flat, by windows painted shut, or immovable because of broken sashes. In a corner a grubby cushion covers a coil of dog-shit, discovered then concealed, and now hardened and crumbly.

'You'd better go,' his sister repeats, as she reaches for the remote control and turns up the volume. He scrunches up the poke and throws it at her. 'Piss off you little shit-head.' She spits out the words in a cautious undertone, but with venom.

'Piss off yerself,' he replies in a near whisper, (there's an unstated rule about noise when dad's conducting his business) and he ducks as she hurls the paper back at him. 'Nyaa, missed me,' and he runs from the room, in case her attempt to chase after him is more than bluff.

His mother, large through a lifetime of fatty food, is lying in bed, though she's fully clothed. There's no carpet on the floor and she turns her head on the pillow at the sound of the hollow beat of his steps on the boards. Piles of clothes spill from the gaping recess that was once a fitted wardrobe; the doors were taken off and used as kindling ages ago, and the clothes rails were removed for some purpose now forgotten. There's a half empty bottle of vodka on a painted wicker cabinet by the bed, and the room smells strongly of body odour and urine. The soiled curtains don't have enough hooks and sag in loops from the runners. They're pulled closed, though the sun is shining outside. The unshaded centre light is on, harshly exposing the room in all its ugliness.

'Oh Jamie, my pet,' she says, and her voice is loaded with the helplessness he knows so well. She stretches out her arm towards him. He wants to turn away at the sight, but at the same time he has to look. She'd cut one of her wrists a couple of days before: hacked away at it with an old razor blade, and his dad had stitched it up with a needle and thread. He was wild. She wouldn't go to the doctor, so he did it. That would teach her, he'd said. Each time she'd shouted out in pain or at the thought of the pain he'd smacked her across the head till she'd just sat there sniffing, in quivering submission and silent tears. He'd made the kids stay in the room while he did it. He doesn't trust anyone. Dad always gets his way. 'Jamie, pet, will you just go to the shop and get me twenty Regal.' She's rummaging in her purse for some money. He can't take his eyes off the stitched up gash. There are purple and yellow blotches around the swollen redness. She sees him looking as she stretches out her other arm with the money held between her fingers.

'Is it sore Mam?'

'No, pet, I've had worse than this, and I've put some stuff on it. I'll be fine.' The "stuff" is neat vodka. 'But I do need the ciggies, Pet.' She looks at him imploringly, hoping he'll do as she asks; mostly he doesn't and she's left helpless and defeated. But this time he takes the money and submits to a kiss as he leans over her. 'Thanks, pet. Twenty Regal, and get yourself something an all.' She pours herself a glass of vodka and sinks back onto the bed. As he leaves his eyes rest for a moment on a picture of Christ; the only attempt at decoration in the room. The picture is called "The Light of the World". The title is printed at the bottom. He's seen it every day for as long as he can remember, and it feels like a central part of his world; a part of his mother which he still associates with soft comforting skin and a distant sweet smell, though the memory of that has all but gone.

The boy goes back through to the living room, where his big brother is now also in the sofa, next to his sister. There's a soap on the television; bronzed and beautiful young families are acting out the dramas of suburban living in the sun. They all have to know whether Susie will find out about Ken's affair with Stefanie. He pauses behind them both till there's a break for the adverts; the shining faces of children posing somewhere in Africa look up towards a jet carrying the Club class.

He leans over and using both hands at once sharply tugs the hair of the two of them, and shoots off amid a cloud of obscenities and out of the door before they can catch him. In the hall the negotiations between his dad and the client are drawing to a close. They both pause to look at him. 'Can't you see I'm busy?' his dad says with an impatient frown, and clips him across the top of his head as he slips out of the door.

They have an understanding with the man in the shop, who turns and reaches down the pack of cigarettes without a flicker of hesitation. 'What's happened to your eye, Jamie?' the man asks him a few minutes later, as he hands over the bag of brightly coloured rubbery looking sweets, which the boy has spent ages choosing through the glass counter. The shop's quiet so the man doesn't mind the time taken.

'Just a fight,' he says.

'Did you win?'

'Oh aye,' he says with pride.

'I'd hate to see the other guy then,' says the man, and they both smile. His dad's always telling him to stick up for himself, and he likes this affirmation of his success.

On the way home he lights up a cigarette, and enjoys the way a woman stops and regards him with emphasised disapproval as he sucks in the smoke, holding the cigarette between thumb and finger like his brother does. He walks slowly, thinking about the morning at school. First his teacher then the school nurse, then the social worker all asking him about his eye, then looking at the bruises on his back. 'I fell,' he'd said, but they kept on asking and asking.

The school nurse had tried to be friendly to him, but then talked about him as if he wasn't there. 'Yes, you see there is definitely the mark of a belt-buckle across his back, do you see?' she'd explained to the headteacher.

Later, he went back to his class, but he knew they'd kept talking about him after he'd gone.

When he gets home from the shop there's a police car parked outside the flats, and he knows it will be something to do with them. Inside there are two policemen and another person, and when she turns as he comes in through the door he sees it's the social worker who asked him all the questions in the morning. The living room is full of people, all shouting or trying to talk at once. As soon as he enters there's a brief lull and he's the centre of attention. His mam has managed to get out of bed and is standing by the bedroom doorway. He goes straight to her and hands her the cigarettes. 'Oh Jamie, you've opened them, you're a naughty boy,' she says in her usual ineffectual tones. Dad glares at her; she's just got no idea. They all look on while she opens the packet with trembling hands, lights a cigarette and takes in a deep draught of the blue smoke, pulling Jamie's head towards her side with her free hand. Then as an afterthought she takes out two more cigarettes and offers them pathetically to the various visitors, who hold up their palms or shake their heads in pitying rejection.

'That's some bruise you've got there wee man,' says one of the policemen. 'How did you come by that then?'

He looks across to his dad for a second before answering. 'I had a fight,' he says, but they're crafty, and the next question is 'who with?' 'Can't remember,' he says, and he knows they think he's lying or stupid. Why do they pick on him?

The policeman laughs. It's all calculated. 'That's a funny thing to forget,' he says.

'Leave the kid alone,' his dad says. 'You've heard what he says.' He sounds calm; he's playing the game. Jamie's mother strokes his hair with quivering fingers.

'Let's just have a wee look at your back, eh Jamie?' and the policeman advances towards him. He moves instinctively behind his mother, and this time his dad moves forwards between them and the policeman. His dad starts going on about this being his house and who do they think they are. You can see the policeman wants him to have a go, so they can have an excuse to lift him. But dad manages to control his anger; he's dealt with the police lots of times before.

Mick had been shut in the kitchen when the visitors arrived, but with the raised voices he becomes more and more excited, and begins to bark incessantly. Jamie's sister goes to settle him down but as soon as she opens the door he pushes past her, and soon he's got the policeman cornered, not the talkative one, the other, silent one, and dad has to quieten it with a well placed kick. The diversion seems to free everything up a bit.

'We've got a warrant,' says the social worker, pulling a sheaf of papers from her handbag. 'Jamie needs to see a doctor so we can get a proper explanation for his injuries.'

Dad looks blank, so she has to explain about the bruises that the P.E. teacher had seen in the morning. 'You looked at my kid without my permission?' His dad takes on the air of injured party, and goes on about knowing his rights and how he'll see his solicitor. They let him have his say. The social worker turns to Jamie's mother. 'You can come as well, of course. It'll be much easier for him if he's with someone he knows.'

'Oh no love, I can't leave the family, I can't leave the house.' And she begins retreating to her bedroom, Jamie still clinging to her.

Dad's weighing things up. 'Piece of bloody nonsense. You've never done nothing for us,' looking at the social worker, 'apart from taking the other yins away,' meaning Jamie's two younger brothers. 'The kid was in a fight, he telt ye.' But you can see he's given in; it's just a gesture. The social worker unfolds some forms, but it feels like provocation: consents to this and that when the child's being taken against their will.

'He'll need some clothes,' the social worker says; 'He'll probably have to stay with foster carers till things have been decided.' But Mam can't manage this, and goes further back into her room. The boy's sister finds a carrier bag and shoves some clothes into it from a drawer in the kids' bedroom. He doesn't understand. He clings to his mother and after they've all stood around for a while, aimlessly arguing, the quiet policeman has to pull them apart and carry him out of the flat, the social worker trying to comfort him by awkwardly holding his hand which is flailing around over the policeman's shoulder. He doesn't know what he's done wrong and he can't see for tears.

Then Mam's in the doorway shouting, 'wait, wait.' For a moment he believes in her, thinks that somehow she's woken up from her apathy at last. But she just thrusts something into his hands then turns and rushes back inside. He can't see what it is because of his tears, and he can't think straight so as to work it out. Can't understand any of it. There's a small group of neighbours gathered round the gate, and they look at him with disapproval. What's he done wrong?

He gets in the back of the police-car with the social worker, and sees that it's the picture from his mam's bedroom that she has given him. The Light of the World. Christ is holding up a lantern which illuminates his face and seems to call him in. It's his mother's face. After they've gone round the corner the talkative policeman puts the siren on for a few seconds to distract him. It works. He feels important, and maybe his dad will be pleased with him, being taken away in a police car. The car is very quiet inside. There's a thrum of silence that separates it from the things they pass, from the familiar noise of the scheme. It smells of newness and something special. The social worker talks to him about what's going to happen. She says they're worried about how he got the bruises, and that a doctor wants to see him and talk about them, and he'll probably be weighed and measured and so on. She says if they're still worried about him after the examination he might have to go and stay with some foster carers for a while till she can talk with his parents about what's to be done. She's nice. But he knows he won't be going home. Just like the twins. They got taken away months ago, and he hasn't seen them since.

*

It's a nice room. Clean. It smells fresh, and the sheets gently crackle as he moves about between them. He's wearing a new pair of pyjamas. They smell unused and sterile. They've taken his own clothes away from him, and he's had a bath and had some stuff put in his hair, that made his scalp go cold and creepy. He played on their computer earlier and they gave him mince and tatties. He couldn't eat the cabbage, but they didn't get cross. They seem very nice, but he doesn't understand why he's here. What's he done wrong? He misses the smell of his own clothes and his house; his mother.

Later on the foster mother comes into the room. 'Hey there, son, what's up with you?' And she takes his hand gently and smiles down at him with concern. For a while he can't speak for sobbing, but then manages to say one word at a time between sobs. 'I.. want.. to.. go.. home. I.. want.. to.. go.. home.' Something is poking out from underneath the pillow. She eases him aside and lifts up the pillow so they can see what it is. It's the picture. His mother's holding the lantern and reaching out to him. But the glass has got broken and sharp cracks radiate in lines from her breast like the impact from a bullet.

7

The Plaited Dog Turd
with the Oak Leaf Sail

There had been warning signs. Like the incident that morning when he had been cleaning his teeth. He'd spat into the basin and a globule of toothpaste (he always used too much), had fallen into the porcelain basin, shined up so white by Cath, and in the spat-up shining bead was a writhing creature; too many legs for an insect, but too limp for a woodlouse, though of course it was water-logged, so even hard casings might soften. Had he coughed it up from his stomach? Like that old woman in Nigeria who claimed to have vomited up a tortoise and had achieved a moment of tabloid fame? He rationalised that of course he hadn't. But where then had it come from? Had it sought refuge from the light in the tube of toothpaste, and been brushed around his mouth? Or fallen from the ceiling, maybe? He looked up, then rinsed it away, then wondered if he'd imagined it, but it was too late. Then, later, there was the dog-turd, beached on the pavement, and plaited, like a girl's pigtail. A mustard-coloured oak leaf, dried by the wind, rose from it like a sail. He'd bent to study it, and passers-by had glanced at him, but he'd had to check. Yes, perfectly plaited, or at least that's what he remembered of it, but things blur as soon as you turn away.

The eventide was blurred, slipping away to emptiness, like in an old movie. It was outside the car, but pressing in, getting closer. He could feel it creeping through the cavities and folds of his body. The opaque air hung in shifting grey layers among the fields, girding the trees which rose above it, their lower trunks half-submerged in the hushed dampness. He peered through the windscreen, on the lookout for the tail-lights of the next car. The hushed grey breath of the evening pressed against the car windows, clouding his senses. The margin of time, the spinning of the earth and the pull of the weak, dying, winter sun, combined to draw his eye time and again, for a piece of a second only, from the road. He felt disconnected from himself, and from the voice on the radio, coming somehow in unseen waves, with the illusion of substance.

He couldn't avoid it when it came, elegantly on tiptoes from the shadow of one of the gateways, its ears held erect. They're always larger than you remember from the time before, maybe because you compare them with rabbits, and like spirits with a hint of something human. It was very quick. The steering wheel shuddered as first the front wheels then the rear wheels struck the poor animal. Th-thum. He could feel the end its life through the steering wheel, and he cried out and braked, but didn't stop. There could be no hope: Th-thum. The sensation he felt through the steering wheel stayed with him, the tremble of the hare's life, which he had taken, made him in turn tremble. The weather forecast on the radio told of the promise of sunshine to come the next day. He could see nothing in the rear mirror, but there could surely be no hope. In his mind he could see it, crouching in spring barley, in the sunshine, its bright, unblinking eyes, full of watchful wildness, the breeze ruffling its soft oatmeal fur. Then writhing in agony on the asphalt, smashed and oozing crimson blood onto the damp, hard, grey road metal. He slowed, almost to a stop, then drew away again, and tuned the radio to a light music station.

*

At home he and Cath watched the news, he swivelling in his special recliner, with his toes stretched towards the coal-effect gas fire. Dad's chair. The evening outside was gone from him now, and had given way to the domestic ritual, both tedious and comforting in its repetitions. The washing-up waited in the kitchen. They couldn't miss the news, which fed them like an intravenous placebo.

'How was your day dear?' not looking at him.

'Fine. Thanks. What about yours?'

'Oh, all right. Sammy fell off his bike, but it's just a graze. Jo went to the dentist. Needs a filling. She eats too many sweets. The window cleaner was in court for assaulting his wife last week. Seems such a nice man. I don't know who we'll get to clean the windows now. You never know about people do you?'

He wondered if she meant him.

'Have you noticed any woodlice about the house?'

'Woodlice?' Her inflexion was scathing. They wouldn't dare. 'I'll buy a spray if you like.'

He couldn't tell her about the hare. He kept thinking about it as he loaded the dishwasher. It was only a hare, he told himself. They ate lambs without a pang, and some folk ate hares. Jugged or something, whatever that meant. He dropped a mug, but it just bounced with a ringing. It's always the ones you don't like that don't break, he thought.

'What was that?' she called from the living room.

'Nothing.' Why does she have to know everything? Life would be more interesting if they had some secrets.

He couldn't sleep that night and got up for a drink of water. The mist had lifted, dispersed by breezes which disturbed the trees. He looked at the moon through the landing window, rising like the dead, unblinking eye of a blind man. It would be reflected off the bloodstained road; the dead touching the dead.

He took a different route next day, to attend a meeting in town before going to the office, but he came back home the usual way. He looked for the body, which by now would be a flattened furry rag, he thought. There were bunches of gaudy flowers in cellophane, like the ones you buy in filling stations from plastic buckets, next to the racks of newspapers. It didn't make sense. There was a teddy bear and other toys, in a pile by the road. Around the corner, where the road widened, there was a police car with a flashing light, two officers in luminous jackets shielding their eyes from the dazzle of his headlights. He stopped and wound down his window.

'Do you usually travel this road at this time of night, sir?'

But before he could answer the second officer called his colleague to the front of the car, pointing to the bumper, bent and dislodged.

He didn't know what they meant when they asked him about the child. He began telling them about the hare, speaking words that were not his own, till he broke down in tears: a child himself. As they talked over their radios the image that for a moment flickered before him, was of the plaited dog-turd with its oak-leaf sail.

8

Learning the Moves

The Snake

Nobody knows about the times Jake got shut in the cupboard under the stairs and was fed from a dog's bowl. He's pushed the memory down into the depths; into a dark place inside him, full of bats and spiders that he mustn't disturb, a place as scary as the cupboard, full of events he no longer recalls. But his times under the stairs and other confusing and terrifying experiences have shaped his view of the adult world and he's as wary as a captured creature which does not know the kindly intents of those trying to care for him. He will never completely heal. Even Taylor, his older sister, doesn't know everything. She'd been removed from home before the really dark times. Then their mum had a new partner and seemed able to cope with baby Jake.

They said she was in a different place. Jake slipped through the net like a little silvery fish.

Jenny is standing on the doorstep. She glances at her watch as the door opens. 'He's waiting for you in the front room,' says Maggie, Jake's foster carer. 'He's in one of his moods because I turned his game off.' Maggie's sleeves are rolled up and she's wiping her pinked-up arms with a faded tea-towel. She looks tired and is putting on weight. She knows she eats too many snacks, but she can't help it; they are a comfort. Jenny, the children's social worker, follows her to the kitchen, watching Maggie's hands kneading the tea towel into a ball. Maggie gives her the latest news; mainly a catalogue of misdemeanours perpetrated by the children. 'We'll chat after I've done some work with Jake,' Jenny says, and heads for the front room. Maggie turns back to the kitchen. There is always a pile of ironing and the air smells of hot linen and fabric conditioner.

Jake's like a little tree-frog; he can launch himself at any time and in any direction. His inscrutable eyes dart about constantly. They have irises of electric blue and pupils like the black opercula of periwinkles. People are worried that his big sister, Taylor, mothers him too much; that she doesn't have enough space to be a child herself and that her close attention is holding them both back. Jenny wants some time with Jake before Taylor gets home from school. Jake ignores her when she first comes into the room but she chats away to him, nevertheless, about her journey and the weather. She's used to his ways. He's squatting, cross-legged, on the fitted oatmeal twist carpet, in front of the grey, lifeless TV screen. Jenny keeps telling Maggie that for sanctions to be effective they have to be balanced with praise. Ten or more positive comments for every reprimand, that's the theory, otherwise children like Jake become impervious to criticism and switch off. But Maggie, well meaning, experienced and skilled as a foster carer, doesn't seem able to sustain it. 'They're just so difficult,' she says. She's worn out.

Jake's reflection, leached and stretched, looks back at him from the grey, flat screen, clear enough for him to see his blond hair and freckles. He can make out Jenny's image beyond his, as she gets the things ready on the table. He wonders if anyone else can see things without looking straight at them. He wants to get back to the safety of World Wrestling Entertainment. He's getting quite skilled at computer games; he gets lots of practise.

Jenny spreads some photographs out on the dining table. It has a childproof washable covering with a bold floral print, smeared with the dried out sweeps of a damp cloth, which shine like snail-trails when caught by the light. These days the table's used for homework, colouring in and piecing lives together. Rarely for eating: that's done in the kitchen in hurried shifts broken by whining complaints. (Mummy, Jake's kicking me under the table again... Taylor called me a cow). Everyone loses their temper with everyone else.

'I've had the photographs printed,' says Jenny, enthusiastically. Jake turns his head slightly, to see if he can trust the picture he sees of her in the background of the TV screen. 'Shall we do some more work on your snake? Match the photographs with the dates?' She clicks open her transparent lime-green attaché case, and the felt-tips and Pritt sticks clatter gently together as she searches for something. Jake can't resist the sound. He turns and rocks himself over to the table, using his arms; springing on his folded legs, before unwinding and climbing on to the chair next to Jenny, gently blowing raspberries as he goes. He laughs at the photographs: a child's innocent, spontaneous laugh that breaks out of a rare natural smile at the sight of his own images smiling up at him from the shiny, coloured flatness; clues to what's lost or buried.

'They're good, aren't they? You're very photogenic, Jake.'

Jake's thumb pushes against the photograph in his hand and it bends and creases. 'Try to hold them by the edges, Jake, or you'll spoil them.' She hears the back door bang shut and Taylor bursts in. 'You've started with out me,' she shouts, dropping her bag and her jacket. 'You can't. What's happening?' She has the same fair hair and freckles as Jake. The same blue eyes.

Jenny explains that she just wanted a bit of time with Jake on her own, but Taylor is having none of it. She's run all the way home, but she wasn't fast enough. Jake bounds over to her. 'It's okay my love,' she says. I'm here.' She looks over to Jenny. 'I saw Mum last week at school,' she says aggressively, 'She's going to get you. We're going back with her to live.' It's not true, of course. None of it.

Taylor comes over to the table and looks down at the pictures, fingering them so they slip and slide over each other like wafers of coloured glass. There's something about the way photographs capture the moment, so that even after years in battered shoe boxes, or creased and bent from being shuffled around among the miscellaneous detritus of untidy drawers, they still bring back a memory, stored in vivid clarity amongst the folds of all that has gone. Not that these pictures are old. There isn't a single photograph in existence of Jake as a baby or a toddler, except for the ones the police took of his bruising: the pink whorls and bluish hand prints on his buttocks.

Jenny tries to make the best of it. 'Come on Taylor. Help Jake glue this one on the snake.' The paper snake is a photocopy of a photocopy, so it's grainy in places and bits of its flat, twisting body are faded and indistinct. It's stuck together with pieces of tape, and once unfolded it stretches the length of the table. It's divided into segments, each representing a slice of

Jake's life; his beginning at the head and his present getting nearer to the tail. Taylor has her own snake. The future is unclear, despite all the time they've spent talking about their new family, and all the videos and photos that have been put together for adoption websites, in which they compete with other smiling children, their hair carefully brushed, or tousled for effect. To Jake and Taylor their new family shimmers, vaguely, like a mirage cast up by the teasing sun on a length of empty road.

Jenny suggests something to write and prints it out for him on a piece of paper. "Fostered by Mr and Mrs Thomson then went back to Mum for a while. Aged three." 'What were the good things about being at the Thomsons, Jake?'

Taylor had been in a different placement then so can't know much about how Jake felt, but she does most of the talking. 'They are the ones who had that dog, aren't they?' she suggests.

'Yes, Nico. Nico was his name,' says Jake. He takes a black felt tip and makes a scribbly black shape on a piece of paper, so vigorously that he makes a hole in the paper and marks the cloth underneath.

'What's this?' asks Jenny gently.

'Rubbish,' he says. 'A bin bag.'

Jenny frowns, not sure what he means.

'They put his stuff in a bin bag when he was moved,' says Taylor. That's what you mean, isn't it, my love?'

Jake nods. Eventually a few more words are added to the snake and Jenny begins packing the things away till next time.

Taylor has calmed down. 'Do you remember last time we had that game, where I had to imagine I was on the end of a rope, dangling over a cliff, and you wanted to know who I would choose to hold the other end and pull me back up?' she asks Jenny.

'Oh yes, you wanted time to think about it.'

'Well I think the best thing would be to just tie the rope to a rock or something like that, a strong tree maybe, then no-one would let go, would they and I could just pull myself up?'

It's not surprising that Taylor doesn't trust anyone. Jenny says something about needing to believe in people, but Taylor shrugs her shoulders and leaves the room. Before she goes Jenny has a word with Maggie in the kitchen to check that she's still able to take the children to the Activity Day coming up on Saturday. 'I'll be there as well, of course,' says Jenny. 'Fingers crossed eh?'

'I don't like these things,' says Maggie. 'Putting them on show. It's like we're going back to the last century, you know when children were sent to Australia and paraded round so they could be chosen by families to work on farms and stuff. Such awful stories.'

Pirates

The Adoption Activity Day takes place in a primary school, otherwise empty at the weekends. The dining hall has been kitted out with "Activity Fun Stations", and children's entertainers are keeping the kids busy making pirate costumes, telling stories and constructing a huge pirate galleon out of scrap cardboard in the centre. There's a faint smell of old cooking and cleaning materials coming through the kitchen hatch, which has been rolled up to provide constant supplies of teas and juice. It's a clear blue-sky day and the doors are open. Jet trails criss-cross like saltires, miles high, taking people on life-changing journeys, but not as life changing as those in the school hall. A gentle breeze stirs the sails of the pirate ship and there is a CD of suitable music... "Fifteen men on a dead man's chest..." There are about twenty children in the hall, and their foster carers and social workers watch them from a distance and step forward to help with a nose-blow or to wipe a chin when need be.

The adoptive families are getting a briefing from the organisers upstairs. Some of their social workers have also come along. Many of the would-be adopters are childless, some are looking to adopt for the second time, one or two have birth children. It's an emotional day. A few of them well-up at the briefing on hearing details of the children they are about to meet. The journey to parenthood has been long and painful for some, with years trying to conceive, unsuccessful IVF, an intrusive adoption assessment and a complicated approval process. 'Just be relaxed, play with them, engage with them, talk to their social workers and foster carers,' they're told. There'll be a de-brief at the end and if there are any children that they're interested in finding out more about they'll be advised about the next steps.

Jake and Taylor are at a table on their own, colouring in a picture of pirates. Taylor is passing Jake the crayons and telling him what to do. Maggie is a little way off, looking at something on her phone. She keeps glancing up to make sure they are okay. The adoptive families move around the hall, engaging with the children and talking to other adults. None of the prospective adopters have been to play with Jake and Taylor yet, and the children are engrossed in their colouring. Jenny has a quiet word with Maggie. 'I think most of the families today are just approved for one child or for children a bit younger than Taylor and Jake, especially Taylor. I had a chat with one couple who said they didn't want to play with them because of that. They didn't want to get the children's hopes up.'

'Never mind, it's a day out anyway. You know my views.' Maggie touches Jenny's arm and steers her into a corner. 'They need to be split up. Taylor sees herself as Jake's mum. They are holding each other back. Separate them. Much better chance.'

'We've been over this, Maggie. They've only got each other. We must try and keep them together. The three siblings are all in different placements.' It is true. Taylor and Jake have an older brother in residential care and two sisters who are each in different foster care placements. They haven't seen them for months.

Half an hour passes. Jake and Taylor move to another table where they are helped by one of the entertainers to make pirate hats. The entertainer has a striped top on and is wearing big earrings and a scarf round her head with a skull and crossed bones design. She keeps calling them "me hearties" and says that they'd better watch their step or they'll have to walk the plank. They are joined by a young man with bright red hair. 'Why are pirates called pirates?' the new arrival asks. 'Because they arrrrrrrr! Where do pirates like to go to have fun? To the Paaaaaark!' Jake giggles, but Taylor's face doesn't crack.

'Hi, I'm Spencer. What are you two up to?' the newcomer asks.

Jake doesn't raise his head, but Taylor looks up. 'Just sticking this stuff,' she says. She looks at Spencer's dyed hair: bright red. 'Are you one of the entertainers?' she asks.

'Me? No, I'm hoping to be a dad one day,' says Spencer.

'Where's your wife?'

'No wife. Just me.'

'Just you?' Taylor looks puzzled. This isn't her idea of a family.

'Yes, that's right.'

The entertainer, makes her excuses and leaves them to talk and play. Maggie is sharing a cup of tea at the other side of the room with a group of other foster carers. Sandwiches, crisps and sausage rolls are being laid out on a table. Taylor fetches Jake a paper plateful and he takes the odd bite.

'Nice hat. What's your name?' ask Spencer.

'His name's Jake,' says Taylor. 'And I'm Taylor.'

'Maybe I can make a hat too?'

Taylor shrugs. 'We're making swords now.' The three of them get stuck in. Spencer doesn't like to ask them too many questions so he rambles on about the films of Pirates of the Caribbean and how the first one was the best. They haven't seen it so he gives a synopsis. The cutting and sellotaping come to a halt as the children listen to his graphic account of pirates turning into skeletons under the deathly grey light of a full moon. He isn't sure he should be telling them this kind of story and he glances around to make sure he isn't being overheard.

He finishes his hat and puts it on. It's not a convincing piece of piratical millinery. Jake laughs at his efforts. 'Shall we get our faces painted?' suggests Spencer. Jake wants to look like a tiger, which isn't really the theme but the face-painter obliges. Spencer becomes a tiger too, out of solidarity. He later realises he is the only adult with a painted face. Taylor decides to stick with the theme and is given a scar and a beard.

'So, are you going to adopt us?' asks Taylor when the face painting is completed. Her directness is disarming. Jake looks up.

'I'm afraid not,' says Spencer. 'I'm just approved to adopt one child. But I've enjoyed being with you.' The children don't seem surprised. After a while Spencer wanders off, still wearing his hat, and has a cup of tea, surveying the hall from a corner on his own.

'I saw you talking to Jake and Taylor. I'm Maggie, their foster carer.' Nice hat. What's with the tiger face though?'

'Oh, you know, just joining in with the spirit of the thing. Lovely kids.'

'Oh yes, nice kids, potentially, but hard work. Exhausting. I don't know how long I can go on.' Maggie goes on to explain something of the children's history. In and out of care. Five different foster care placements. Her view that they need to be separated to have any chance.

'It would be such a shame if they couldn't be together,' he says.

'There's no chance,' she replied. 'They've been waiting for two years. It'll soon be too late for either of them to be adopted. Once they reach school age adoption's practically out of the question. And of course Taylor is nearly eight already. Jake will be five in a few months.'

'Then what?' Spencer takes a sip of tepid tea. He is nervous and it slops into the saucer.

'Permanent foster care I should think. Probably separate placements. You seemed to get on well with Jake...'

Hobnobs

Spencer doesn't sleep that night, agonising about whether he should make an offer to adopt Jake; take it to the next level. He comes to a decision at 3.30 a.m., and wanders around his flat picturing *both* children in their bedrooms and having meals with him around the kitchen table. The next day he phones his social worker, and tells her about Jake and Taylor. 'Oh, yes, I know of them,' she says. 'Sorry I couldn't make it to the Activity Day. But you're only approved for one pre-school, Spencer; the plan is for Jake and Taylor to be together and Taylor is nearly eight years old.'

'I felt a connection,' he says. They talk for a while. Spencer is a determined young man. He has doggedly pursued his adoption application against all the odds; there aren't many single, gay male adopters around. Eventually she agrees to phone the children's social worker, to test the water.

'The young man with the dyed hair and the tiger face? Oh yes, I remember seeing him.' Jenny had been excited when the call first came through, but her excitement soon flips over to disappointment. 'We're really looking for a two parent family for Jake and Taylor,' she says flatly. She says she'll give it some consideration, but doesn't give it any further thought till she has supervision with her team leader the following week.

'Any luck with the Activity day for Jake and Taylor,' she is asked. They are sharing a cafetière of Machu Pichu fair trade and the team leader has a packet of biscuits at the ready.

'Just an enquiry from this really young guy. He's only approved for one, so it would be complicated anyway. He might be okay for Jake, but he wouldn't manage Taylor. He's so young, and he has red hair. It's a non-starter.'

'I didn't have you down as someone who might be prejudiced against gingers!'

'No. It's dyed red. Bright red. He's gay. Gay but single. I'm sure he's very nice, but not for Taylor and Jake.'

'There's nothing in the regulations about not placing children with adopters who dye their hair. There isn't exactly a queue of families interested in Jake and Taylor. And the placement they're in isn't going to last much longer.'

'It wouldn't work. He can't be more than thirty.'

But her team leader takes the role of devil's advocate. 'What does Spencer's social worker think? What support does he have. Being young he might have lots of energy. What other options are there?

'Maybe he could just adopt Jake, maybe that would be more realistic?'

'And what would happen to Taylor? I'm just saying, think it over. I know you want the ideal family for them, but it's not going to happen. We need to think outside the box. She pauses; it's her job to challenge. 'Would you like a Hobnob?' She tears away the packaging and holds out the cylindrical arrangement of biscuits in a way that is irresistible, and they go on to discuss the rest of Jenny's caseload.

Jenny does think it over. She knows Jake and Taylor need two parents who will have the time to give them individual attention; to allow Taylor to stop being a mother to Jake, to give her a childhood, to survive. But she phones Spencer's social worker nonetheless. 'He's irrepressible,' she's told. Unusual: a single gay man wanting to adopt. Some eyebrows raised, you can imagine, but he's sound; determined to be a parent. It's been a long road for him. When he first enquired he didn't have the space, so we told him to come back when he had a bigger place to live. And back he came. Attended all the training sessions. He's youthful; only thirty-one, though he looks even younger. One of the most open-minded adopters I've ever met. And I've seen him with his nephew. Bags of energy and full of ideas. I agree, this is a big step, though, taking on siblings. How about if I introduce you?'

They go to his flat a couple of weeks later. Spencer gives Jenny a tour. Two bedrooms and a box room with only an internal window.

'I don't think a box room would meet our standards. And they've got to have separate rooms.'

'Oh, I'll sleep in there,' he replies, then adds: 'I'm not in a relationship at the moment, and I have no plans. Parenthood is my priority.'

Jenny nods inscrutably. The flat isn't like something from Ideal Home, but it's fine: bright colours, Ikea furniture, his nephew's paintings on the wall. There is a smell of coffee and baking bread. It's like he's trying to sell the flat to them, which in a way he is.

'And what do you do, Spencer?'

He tells her he works as a chef at Giovanni's. 'But I'll take a year off,' he adds.

They talk and talk. Once Jenny has asked all the questions she has about him, she takes a breath and tells him about Jake and Taylor. They both have what she calls developmental uncertainty. Jake is thought to have Foetal Alcohol Spectrum Disorder as a result of his mother's drinking during pregnancy. Taylor has attachment difficulties, but is quite bright. They have experienced lots of trauma and change. Their father is serving a life sentence for murder. Their mother is in a new relationship but is still using drugs and is pregnant again. There are three other siblings, all to different fathers and all in different placements. They have occasional contact. The story becomes more and more grim. He is told about the bruising to Jake, picked up during a visit from the Health Visitor. Spencer listens. He's heard all about this type of thing at the training sessions, but he's met these kids and it is a shock hearing what they'd been through, and to hear them described in clinical terms.

'We've been thinking that we maybe need to review the plan, that they might need to be placed separately. There'd probably be more interest in Jake on his own and we should be able to find another foster placement for Taylor. We might be able to consider you for Jake if you're interested?'

'You're the professionals,' says Spencer. 'But from what I've seen, you can't split them up. You just have to see them together. They need each other.'

'Let's leave it there today,' says Jenny. 'We can all think things over and talk again in a day or two.'

Tap Dancing

A few weeks pass. Jenny's initial resistance to Spencer's offer to adopt both children softens. The adoption agency reviews Spencer's approval and after much discussion adjust it so he can take siblings. There are lots of meetings: adoption panels, children's hearings, linking meetings, matching meetings. It is bewildering, but Spencer comes through it all. He is determined on the outside and knows this is something he has to do. He feels there is no going back now. But on the inside he's scared. He is given lots of information about Taylor and Jake. Taylor is into tap dancing, so Spencer's sister introduces him to her friend who teaches him some steps; a crash course on Tap. They work in his kitchen. He's bought special steel-tipped shoes.

'Okay step one,' she says. She holds his hand and stands beside him. She is wearing shorts so he can see her feet. 'Give me toes. Toe, toe, toe, toe.' She taps away on his laminate and he copies her. 'Now step two: heel, heel, heel, heel. Right and left, right and left. Now bend the left knee and tap to the right side: tap, toe, tap, toe, one two three four five six seven eight. Now brush and drag, brush and drag...' They tap away for an hour. 'Not bad,' she says. 'You need to learn the moves. Practise every day now, you hear?' I can give you another lesson next week.'

He asks her how much.

'Oh, no charge, I like what you're doing. And you're fit. Has anyone ever told you? Shame you're gay. No second thoughts about that I suppose?' They laugh. She kisses him on the cheek when she leaves.

Spencer learns that Jake likes WWE so he buys the computer game and spends hours getting to know the stars: the Undertaker, John Cenar, Randy Orton,

Stephanie McMahon. It's a different world. He learns how to fight on screen. It is as challenging as the training sessions he'd attended at the adoption agency; no matter how hard he tries the figures seem to have minds of their own. He wonders of it's an allegory to what lies ahead when the children move in. He meets up with Maggie for a detailed discussion about what it's like to care for the children. He feels she doesn't like him; that she thinks he won't be able to do this.

'Have they told you Jake wets the bed nearly every night?' She asks. 'And that he sometimes bangs his head? Deliberately.' She seems to go out of her way to be discouraging. They hadn't told him these things. 'Oh, yes,' he says. I've got a good washing machine.' He wonders what else they haven't told him.

You'll Never Be My Dad

'So you're going to be our new Dad?' says Taylor.

'Well maybe. What do you think of that?'

'You'll never be *my* Dad,' she says. Never. Do you hear me? I don't need a dad. But I'll come so I can look after Jake. He seems to like you.' She is like a cross between a fishwife, a school dinner lady and the little girl she is meant to be.

On a later visit Spencer persuades her to show him her tap dancing. They have to go into the kitchen, off the carpet. Kitchens and tap dancing seem to go together. Maggie clears away the ironing board and watches from the doorway as Taylor begins her moves. After a while he joins in. Taylor's mouth falls open and she stops dancing while he completes his routine and finishes with arms splayed out and a broad grin. He is almost as good as she is. 'Course I'm better when I'm wearing the right shoes,' he says. 'What do you think?'

'You need to practise,' she says, rather stony faced. It isn't the reaction Spencer had been hoping for.

Welcome Gifts

After all the waiting, the interminable processes, checks and assessments, the children move in surprisingly quickly after a few introductory visits. Spencer collects them in his car. They are high with excitement. Maggie waves them off in tears, but they don't seem to notice. Spencer has bought welcome gifts: a framed piece of "genuine wrestling ring canvas" from the WWE for Jake, signed by his hero, John Cenar, which cost a fortune, and a sparkly dancing outfit for Taylor. They hardly look at them. They explore the flat, their new forever home, as Jenny has described it to them, then sit on the sofa wondering what next, with Spencer in an armchair also wondering what next. He resorts to WWE games for Jake eventually, and gets Taylor to help him warm pizzas in the oven. It all feels like a huge anti-climax. At bedtime Jake becomes inconsolable, sobbing because he wants to be back with Maggie, who to all intents and purposes has been his mother for the last two years. Spencer tries everything: a Disney film, more wrestling games, ice-cream, a promise that they will see Maggie soon, but nothing seems to help. Even Taylor's hug and 'come on my love,' doesn't work. Eventually Jake cries himself into a state of exhaustion and Spencer puts him to bed, arranging all his cuddly toys around him. Taylor gets into bed with him, and Spencer sits on the floor beside the bed, alternately reading stories and singing silly songs till the three of them fall asleep.

Say Cheese

The next few months are the hardest of Spencer's life. The children continue to grieve for Maggie. They meet up with her from time to time and they are always distressed when they part. 'You need to stick with it,' Spencer's social worker tells him. 'They need to process their feelings. Better in the long run.' Spencer isn't convinced but does as he is advised. He was told they might not show much affection for a while. Then he was told they might never show much affection because their ability to make attachments had been severely damaged by their early experiences. He learns to count to ten when things get tough; Taylor in particular seems to know which buttons to press. He tries to give the ten points of praise for each criticism as he has been advised to do. 'They have fragile self esteem,' Jenny says. 'Don't turn into a nag or you won't get anywhere.' He constantly feels he's failing. Taylor seems to take a delight in undermining him. 'You should know by now that Jake doesn't like his cheese on top of the pasta; he needs it on the side... I don't think Jake is taking to you at all; he needs a mum...Maggie used to buy Heinz beans not this junk...' One night she says, 'This isn't working out, is it? Are we going back into foster care?'

'Just go to bed Taylor, just go to bed.' He's close to his limit. She bangs her bedroom door and he finds himself crying.

Spencer turns to friends, his sister, his mother and even the tap dancing teacher for help. They give him breaks and say the right things to keep him going. He goes to a support group run by the adoption agency for adoptive parents, and finds the issues he's wrestling with are shared by many. It makes things feel better and he learns from the other parents, who also learn from him. 'What do you think Dad would've made of this, Mum?' he asks one day as his mother is tackling a pile of ironing. She irons quietly for a few moments before saying, 'I think he'd be very proud, son.' Spencer smiles. He hadn't had an easy relationship with his dad, who even at the time he died had not come to accept him for who he was.

The adoption application, the formal legal process, takes over a year to come to court. Spencer still has doubts; sometime he feels as if they are in a boat without oars going down a rapidly flowing river. Maybe it will get easier after the adoption comes through, he thinks. Maybe we'll all feel more relaxed then? Everyone keeps telling him how well he is doing; how the children are beginning to settle. And there are good signs; Jake hardly ever wets the bed now.

When the big day comes, he and the children are ushered into the judge's chambers. The judge is friendly. 'In the old days it was always middle class people who adopted, and it was always babies,' she says to Spencer. He wonders what she is going to say next. She is looking at the children who are at the other side of the room trying on her wig and giggling. 'It's all so different now. Thank goodness! You seem to be doing a great job.' She bends over her desk and signs some papers. She's read all the reports.

'Can we take a photo?' asks Spencer, 'so we can have something to look back on.'

The judge agrees and the clerk takes a picture of them all together. 'Say Cheese,' he says, trying to work out which part of Spencer's phone to touch to capture the moment, and they all laugh.

They have to weave in and out of police officers, accused persons and lawyers in gowns as they leave the court and step outside. They pick their way through groups of nervous smokers. Jake is holding Spencer's hand and he gives it a squeeze. They smile at each other. Taylor is slightly apart, as she always is. A woman approaches them. She is all in black, dressed as if for a funeral. 'Hello Taylor, Jake,' she says. 'I didn't want you to think I didn't care.' She takes off the sunglasses she is wearing so they can see her more clearly, but in so doing exposes a black eye. The children move behind Spencer. 'I'm their mother,' she says to him. Spencer wonders what is coming next. He glances over his shoulder to check if there is a spare police officer anywhere around. His heart is pounding. But she is harmless; there is something broken about her. Spencer can smell drink, even though they are some way apart. 'It's all right,' she says. 'It's just, well, I didn't want you to think I didn't care, you know? I'm not here to make any bother. I just wanted to see you.' They stand awkwardly for a few moments and tears begin to run down her cheek, blurring her mascara. 'I'm sorry,' she says, trying to catch the children's look. 'Sorry for everything. He's away now,' she continues, 'Got lifted a couple of days ago. A new start, for all of us, eh? It's better this way. I just wanted to say...I love you. I love you both. I just wanted to see you.' The children keep hiding behind Spencer. They are all fixed, like a tableau, then Spencer moves towards her and gives her a hug. 'Take care,' he says. 'I'll write to you: let you know how they're getting on.' She smiles. 'C'mon kids,' he says.

They walk away, Taylor and Jake twisting periodically to look back at her, till they turn the corner.

They go to Giovanni's later that day to celebrate. Giovanni and the others are pleased to see Spencer and he introduces them to the children. 'I hardly recognised you with your new hair,' says Giovanni. Spencer has dyed it blonde, the same colour as that of Jake and Taylor. Spencer is going to start back at work doing lunches in a couple of weeks, now that Jake has started school. 'Yes, good hair, Spencer, much better than that red you had. These children of yours are a good influence on you. We won't have to hide you and your red hair in the back, away from the customers any more!'

'It was Jake's idea' says Spencer. 'I thought we could all go bright blue, but he and Taylor weren't keen for some reason.'

They all laugh. 'Now we really would have to keep you out of sight with blue hair!'

'Hey, don't you be rude about my dad,' says Jake.

'He's my dad as well,' Taylor rebukes. 'And his hair is cool, so there.'

Spencer bends over the menu but can't quite make out any of the words.

9

The Orange Buoy

She leans into the crook of his arm; her long fair hair lying against him in a wave, just like her mother's, but tangled after their busy day. It needs a good brush. She smells of the sea and of sunshine. Her hair is full of sand where they had rolled down the dunes. They can shower in the morning, he thinks; forget the rules today. He holds her gently and presses his cheek to the top of her head. He doesn't hold anyone else now. There is comfort for them both. She can't hold back a yawn, her mouth pulling wide despite her efforts to keep it closed. May, and the long day keeps stretching onwards and onwards. The evening fades slowly, the colours of the landscape leaching into tones and the pink-washed undersides of the slowly processing clouds fill the picture window as they roll over the rented cottage. There is a clicking sound as the electric radiator heats up; the noises and quirks of the little house have become familiar over the days. He has moved the sofa near to the window so they can look out across the falling away fields to the sea beyond; the white horses breaking the surface and dying.

His rearrangement of the furniture means the rest of the room looks disturbed and out of kilter. Spring seems late. The trees and shrubs, slanting and stunted by years of winter winds, are not yet fully green, but the leaf buds are loosening, unfurling slowly, amid electric smears of a million bluebells stretching across the fields. Apart from the clicking, the sound is of birdsong; a blackbird now on the crown of an alder and nearer the shore the mournful cry of curlews, and the alarmed piping of oyster catchers, like piccolo players, somewhere, unseen. He pictures them with quivering wingbeats, moving low and level over the restless water and the black volcanic rocky shore. Oh to fly.

Earlier, they had heard a cuckoo. Shh, listen, he had said, as it called to them both, its notes growing and fading on the breeze across the fields; a rare thing. They had shared the thrill of excitement and exchanged their knowledge of its cruel and tenuous life-cycle, hoping it would succeed in secreting its egg, so that, as she said, her grandchildren would hear it too; she must have read a book or a poem; she was always reading. They skimmed over the blind chick's murderous ways. But he was pleased. Her mother had liked being outside, as long as she had the right footwear and a tasteful hat, but she'd lacked his passion for the living, breathing natural world, whilst Ginty seemed to have inherited that gene from him, or absorbed his enthusiasm. Together they had watched a hen harrier quartering on the still brown hill and counted gannets plunging into the slate blue-grey sea, always pushing their wings back just in time, no matter how often you looked and wondered if this time they would fail. They had been so close to goldfinches that they could see the white spots on their tails. It was Ginty who had first seen the hare as they ate egg sandwiches near the broch.

I saw it first, didn't I Dad? she had said, leaping up and frightening the curlews so they took to the air in shrieking alarm. I saw it first.

Yes, Ginty, you saw it first. She'd glowed with pleasure. Walking back along the rough potholed shore, she had taken his hand and hummed a tune of her own composition.

An early May evening; the night settles slowly here. The pace of their lives has decelerated, but when the time comes to leave it will be almost as if they'd never been. Now they are waiting for the first flash of red.

She yawns again. 'Maybe it's time for bed?' he suggests teasingly.

'Oh Dad, you promised. I'm not really tired. Just, you know, a little bit. But we're on holiday, aren't we?'

'Yes, okay,' he says. They resume their waiting. He can feel her anticipation, her excitement over such a small thing.

'I wish we were always on holiday.'

'We'd get fed up eventually.'

'I would have thought it was dark enough now, Dad,' she says. It is a kind of question.

'It's hard to say,' he replies; a father's evasive answer.

Things are not certain. The light will be activated by a sensor when the time is right. During the day blue and white boats, rocking on the crumpled sea, had brought divers to explore the wreck beneath the buoy and shine their lights on conger eels, their primaeval eyes staring out of fissures, and starfish and the other secret sea creatures that had claimed the broken ghostly ship as their home. The slowly rolling orange buoy had drawn people towards it to sink below the skin of the Sound. But now, as night comes, there is a need to warn off the ships and the tacking yachts that cut laboriously through the Sound.

They sit quietly on the sofa, waiting for the daylight to die and the red light that will come in two pulses. You can stay up till the light comes on, he had agreed. It was way past her usual bedtime. But he hopes the light will not come yet; he needs the comfort of her leaning against him; her vulnerable, dependent breathing form; the reassurance that things are getting better for them both. Please not yet.

'Mum was with us last time,' she says, breaking the quietude. 'Do you think she would have made me go to bed?'

He tenses and crosses his legs. 'She always wanted what was best for you, Ginty.' Sometimes he feels like a therapist. It's like an act. He says things he doesn't feel.

She twists about, snuggling closer; she isn't fully aware. He doesn't know how much she really knows, how much to tell her. He strokes her hair. 'You'll have to have a shower in the morning; your hair is full of sand. What an irresponsible father I am.'

'It was worth it though, wasn't it, Dad?'

'Yes, it was worth it,' he says quietly after a moment.

She'd rolled down the dunes squealing with the thrill of the twisting, turning world, and made him roll too. Too old for this, he'd thought, standing dizzily afterwards, feeling queasy with the sky spinning. He too has sand in his hair. After the world had settled they had walked along the strand turning over straps of khaki coloured kelp, torn from the ocean's floor and stranded on the high water mark. Sand-hoppers had bounced around like bubbles from a fizzy drink.

Now they sit. The fish and chips they had eaten earlier keep repeating and he burps.

'*Dad!*' she says, in mock outrage, just like her mother would have done.

'Better out than in,' he responds. A quote from Fantastic Mister Fox, an old favourite, one of several they quote from between themselves, and they both laugh. They keep their eyes fixed on the buoy, waiting for the first awakening light. She yawns again. I want to see the first one, Dad, she'd said, we mustn't miss it. Okay, Ginty, we'll watch for it together, he'd agreed.

He yawns too. 'Look, you've got me doing it now!' He gets up to pour himself a whisky.

'No Dad, come on, be quick, what if I miss it?'

'Just keep watching,' he says quietly.

But she is worried, close to tears. She cries at the slightest thing. 'What if I'd missed it?' she asks, when he comes back. 'I don't like it when you drink whisky.'

'It's fine. Just a wee one, Little-Miss-Worry-about-Everthing.' He gives her a friendly poke in the ribs and she squirms.

They watch for minute longer. Still no light. 'See, we haven't missed it, have we?'

'I need to see it; the first one,' she says.

'What is so important about it, Ginty?'

'It's the first one, Dad; it's special.'

'Okay, okay. It won't be long now.' He sips his whisky and a wave of pleasure runs through him.

'I'll try not to wet the bed tonight, Dad.'

'It doesn't matter. The rubber sheet's on and there's plenty of clean sheets. It was a good drying day. There's no problem, okay?'

She nods, snuggling into him.

The orange light buoy is half way across the Sound, but from their window it looks close in to the shore because of the lie of the land and the position of the house. It is larger than it looks from where they sit. While they were eating their egg sandwiches on the shambles of the ruined broch a shag had stood upon its gently bobbing summit, drying its outstretched wings. Ginty was full of questions on their walk. What were they like; the people who built the broch? When did they live here? What did they do all day? Did the children go to school? He told her all he knew, with the elastic prerogative to which parents are entitled. They were Iron Age people, who lived about the same time as Jesus. They probably caught fish and kept animals. They used the sea to get from place to place in wooden boats. They probably thought and felt about things the same way that we do. Did they have socks? she had asked. I bet it was cold in the winter. Imagine no chocolate. Did Jesus come here, do you think?

The broch is hidden behind the trees in the fading light. He vaguely wonders now about the people who built it and the generations who lived there, the contrast with the order of the Roman Empire in this distant edge of rocky land. What did they think about as they looked up at the stars, the same stars? He wonders what sense they made of the standing stones up the hill, placed perhaps thousands of years earlier.

'It was my fault Dad, wasn't it?' She says quietly.

'What?' He is miles away. He has heard her but doesn't know what to say. He knows what she means.

'What happened to Mum; it was because of me. Because of the things I said when she was ill that time. I should have understood. I should have behaved better.'

119

'Ginty, of course it wasn't your fault. You didn't say anything.' He pulls her towards him and hugs her. 'Things happen. She was, how can I put it? She was lost, pulled in different directions. And things sometimes happen, and it just isn't fair, but we have to get on with life. We have to remember the good times.' He tries hard to sound strong and sure. It's important that he sounds strong and sure.

She falls silent, thinking. He wonders if she's dropping off. But then she speaks again. 'I don't understand it all, Dad. How could she do that to herself.'

'It was a sort of accident, Ginty. Sometimes we can't just explain everything.'

They sit, waiting for the light. He gets up and opens the window so that they can hear the blackbird. A cool breeze plays with the curtains, but they need the bird's song inside the room, or at least he does, and he hopes that Ginty does too.

'I'm glad she left us her paintings and drawings,' she says.

There is a large portfolio of the drawings in the spare bedroom at home. Ginty keeps undoing the tapes that hold them together and looking at them, searching for traces of her mother; for messages, for clues in the thick, charcoal covered paper. He watched her from the doorway once, turning the pictures this way and that, studying them like an art critic. He wants to get up for another whisky, but he doesn't move. If it hadn't been for the art class she wouldn't have met Simon. But she would have met somebody else; it was inevitable. He can't get rid of the memory of seeing them in bed together when he came home unexpectedly from work. It was like a scene from a soap opera, but just for a moment. She'd looked up and seen him and all he could do was turn around again and leave the house. He will never forget the look on her face; as if she was falling and knew he could not catch hold of her. It was the last time he saw her before the accident. He has to call it an accident.

'Some of the people have no clothes on Dad. Have you seen them?'

'Yes, I've seen them. It's fine. The human form is beautiful.'

'I don't think it's very nice. I think it's just rude! Why did Mum draw those things?'

'It's fine, Ginty.' He rubs her arm and she snuggles closer. The minutes pass and the light fades imperceptibly, the colour of the clouds flushing deeper before the coming of the semi darkness; the sky will retain a flush of daylight till the sun returns.

'Maybe it's broken? Maybe the light isn't working,' she says after a while.

'I think it'll be okay – it's all controlled from an office in Edinburgh or London or somewhere. It's all on their computer. They'll know if it needs fixed and send someone. Just keep watching. Any minute now, I bet.'

Time passes and the blackbird continues with its fruity song. It is answered by another. There is stillness for a time, then from nowhere a gentle movement of the branches, such as the people of the broch would have seen. The minutes pass and the years have passed. Faint lights flicker in the houses across the Sound, quivering because of the shifting air bending their photons. The distant barking of a dog carries over the water. Ginty reaches for the book they had bought in the morning: The Life of St Columba.

'Will you read to me before bed, Dad?' She asks.

'We did agree that you'd go to bed straight away, once we've seen the light, because it's so late.'

'Just one chapter. Pleeeeease Dad.' She draws out the word the way pleading children do.

He keeps her in suspense for a few seconds. 'Okay. One chapter.'

It had been a brief distraction. When they look up the light flashes once, twice, then there is a pause for fifteen seconds, then twice more.

Ginty gasps. 'Was that the first flash, Dad, was that the first?' She's up at the window.

'Yes, it must have been,' he says.

'But was it really? Are you sure?'

He can't be certain. He can't lie. 'I think so, but it doesn't really matter, does it?'

'Yes, it does matter, it does.' She gets to her feet. She is upset. 'Things never work out for me. I wanted it to be right this time.' She is crying.

'It's only a light,' he says. 'An automatic light, triggered by a sensor. It doesn't matter.'

She turns from the window and looks at him, her silhouette against the still pale sky outside. 'Sometimes you don't understand things like Mum does, Dad.' She is crying quietly. 'I wish she was here.' She's so far away, in just a few seconds.

'I know, love,' he says. He holds out his arms and she falls into them. He kisses the top of her head. 'How about if we look again tomorrow? Now off to bed with you. Clean your teeth, brush your hair and I'll come and read that chapter to you in five minutes.'

She takes the book and quietly leaves the room. His glass is empty but he tilts it back so a final drop of whisky slides into his mouth, pricking his tongue, and he looks out across the Sound at the pulsing light; two beats then a pause, like a silent heartbeat among the shorebirds' song.

10

Susie's Song

'Elspeth?' His voice resonates off the veneered door in the confined space just outside the bathroom. He waits for a moment in the silence that follows. She must be in there; the door is locked. They never lock the door; hardly ever close it, except when Elspeth is having one of her occasional foam baths by candle-light.

'Elspeth?' he repeats. He can hear something; a faint crackling of plastic as she tears open the packaging.

'Yes?' she answers wearily.

'What are you doing in there?'

'What do you think?'

He hesitates, uncertain. 'Susie's awake.'

He's so close to the door his breath comes back to warm his face. He stands there, bent over; head tilted, his hand floating uncertainly above the door handle. He glances at his moccasin slippers. It's always slippers and dressing gowns on Sunday mornings.

'Elspeth?'

'Yes, I know, Frank,' she says shortly. Her tone conveys resentment, which hangs in the artificial pine-scented air.

Frank hadn't slept well. In the middle of the night he'd found himself thinking of the paperboy. 'You'll have to say something to him,' Elspeth had said shortly. 'The supplements were practically unreadable last week. It's always me, who has to sort everything out isn't it? I have to do everything.' Frank doesn't like conflict, but he's ready to tackle the paper boy. He's rehearsed what he's going to say.

'I'll make some coffee.' He's talking to the closed door. 'Elspeth?' His voice lifts in enquiry.

'Right. I'll be out in a minute.'

'Would you like some toast?' She doesn't answer. He waits for a second then goes into Susie's room. Elspeth can hear them; the soundproofing in the house is awful. 'How's Daddy's little sweetheart? How's my little baby, then?' Susie is standing up; holding onto the rails of her cot. She beams at him, then falls back onto her bottom and grabs a cuddly toy; Benji, the puppy with the long ears and the so-soft fabric is her favourite. She thrusts it up towards Frank; she has so much to give. Frank throws back the curtains and the slanting yellow sun bursts into the pink-washed room. A thin wall separates them from Elspeth, but they could be on another continent.

They had never thought that they wouldn't be able to have children. They had successful careers; they were *professionals*. They'd bought a house with children in mind, with a garden that happened to have a climbing frame in it already, and a good school just a few minutes walk away. Three good sized bedrooms. The previous owners didn't mention the poor soundproofing of course. Then months of trying. It's an odd word to use; *trying*. Trying for a baby. Sex became stressful. They were desperate for a baby. They would work out the best time, almost to the nearest hour, and Elspeth would thrust at Frank so aggressively in her sweaty, naked desperation that he was almost scared. But nothing happened and the months went by and it was so, so slow. It didn't help when Frank's mum said things like: *no sign of starting a family yet, then?* And Elspeth just had to smile as if it was a huge joke. *You need to watch the biological clock*. Elspeth didn't need telling. She needed a baby; it was her reason for living.

It was all so unfair. A girl, Kate, came to clean the house twice a week at times when Elspeth worked at home. She brought her baby with her; a cute little thing called Marc, who rolled around on the floor while Kate glided about the carpets with the Dyson, polished the wooden surfaces and plunged a bristly brush about in the toilet. Elspeth fell in love with Marc. Kate would come into the room to find that Elspeth had abandoned her laptop and was letting Marc hold her finger. Kate was so proud of him. She once said, laughing, that Marc was an accident. Elspeth watched her feed him from a bottle, and once or twice Kate let her hold him while she did some ironing. Elspeth let Marc snuggle against her; she wouldn't have given him formula milk if he had been hers. She had a fantasy that he *could* be hers. She once asked Kate if she had any regrets. 'I wouldn't part with him for anything,' Kate had said. Elspeth had forced a smile.

Then, after years of humiliating medical procedures, during which hopefulness turned to loss, they plucked a baby from China. It wasn't as simple as that of course. It turned out it was Frank's fault; that he had a low sperm count. The consultant said it was possible they could conceive, with a lot of luck, but very unlikely. They thought about a donor, but then decided on adoption: equal partners, they thought. A social worker visited them over a period of months, asking about their childhoods, their relationship, previous relationships. They had to scrape around for evidence of their ability to look after children; tricky when you don't have any! They needed references, they had to have medical examinations; it seemed to go on for ever. Each week Kate would come to do the cleaning, bringing Marc with her, a toddler now, and not quite so sweet; an unplanned accident, for which there had been no assessment about suitability to parent. How unfair is that? Elspeth used to think. But they got through it at last. Then everything had to be translated and approved in China. It wasn't for the faint hearted!   But then one day she was in their arms: a healthy, rosy-cheeked, unwanted girl, ready to mould, with no history, from a factory-like orphanage in a grey, smoky city full of spinning bicycles and tall buildings under construction. It was like a dream. She was handed over in a hotel room, the ubiquitous sort that could just as easily be Glasgow, except for the sweetish smell of conditioned air and open drains, and they were signing papers. Into her arms, to be precise. A baby who was so clean that her skin shone, writhing about in a nest of white cotton. True, she had a hair lip, but that could be sorted. The days of adopting from China were coming to an end; older girls, disabled children; that's all there were; the rest are adopted in China itself. They were so lucky. On that first day all she seemed to want was food; formula milk.

They'd been on a bus tour of the city the day before, with German tourists who grumbled about the quality of their breakfasts, and who filmed the fish market on their phones. Then their baby was delivered the next morning at 11.15a.m. It was a business-like hand-over.

They'd tried to adopt here of course, but the lists were closed for babies, and they knew they couldn't manage the sort of older, traumatised children who were up for adoption; Elspeth needed to love and to be loved in return. But she had doubts from the moment she saw her; from the moment she'd felt the heat of her body through the white blanket that enveloped her. It was what they'd always wanted; it would come right later, but it felt like her feet had no purchase on the icy slope. It will take time, she'd thought. She wondered if Frank had doubts too, but she doubted it. He was besotted. She didn't speak of it, but months later it still wasn't how she thought it would be. It was a cultural revolution. During their assessment by the adoption agency they'd met adoptive parents who described feeling love at first sight when they were introduced to their child; *I love her to bits*, said one mother, welling up at the memory, though there were others who said it took a while and for some it was still work in progress. But this baby was a stranger to Elspeth. She couldn't admit that she didn't love her little Susie the way she should, but it was hard keeping up that level of pretence. The doctor said it was a bit like post-natal depression; that long slow build up; the incredible emotional investment; the crashing anti-climax. *It's a wonderful thing you've done,* she said. *Give it time and take these pills.* And she *is* getting there, but it's a lonely journey. Susie is perfect; Elspeth even loves her hair lip; the problem is *her*, she thinks. Give it time. They've waited for years, but she needs to give it time.

And now? What is she doing in the bathroom? She's sitting on the toilet holding a glass of her warm yellow urine. Take a mid-stream sample the instructions read.

It's dribbled over her hands, but she's made no move to wash them. It's simple enough: she has to dip the end into the sample and if the test is positive a plus sign will appear in the second window. It will mean that one of Frank's lonely little sperm will miraculously have hit the bullseye. It seems curious that the sweet, warm waste, filtered out of her blood, will hold the answer. She licks a drip from the back of her hand, and as she does her eye catches the net of Susie's plastic toys strung over the hook on the back of the bathroom door. The plastic duck's yellow head presses against the white mesh through which its bill has broken.

She can hear Susie singing in her room. She's so musical, even at this age; beautiful wordless songs. She's pulled the string on her musical rabbit; a present from Frank's brother and his wife; everyone was so pleased for them.

Frank is looking through the muslin curtains of the bay window in the living room. He sees the paperboy working his way along the street, wheeling a trolley because of the weight of the Sunday supplements. He goes through to the hall and opens the front door just as the boy comes up the path. 'Hi,' he says. The boy has his Ipod plugged in and doesn't hear at first. 'Can I just say,' Frank begins, 'that the last couple of weeks the papers have got ripped coming through the letterbox. Maybe you could just ring the doorbell to save you from having to ram them in eh?'

'They're just so thick,' explains the boy.

'That's why I'm suggesting you ring the bell. Is that okay? Sorry, what's your name?'

'Logan. Aye, no problem. I'll ring in future. Here you go then.' He hands Frank the papers.

'Hope you don't mind me mentioning it?'

'No, you're okay. Cheers then.' He heads down the path, adjusting his earphones as he goes.

Frank watches him go. Logan; his whole life in front of him. Not a care in the world. Elspeth hears the front door close and the rustle of papers; Frank is scanning the headlines.

'Elspeth?' he calls from the foot of the stairs. He sounds so far away from where she sits in the bathroom. 'Coffee's ready. And the papers are here. All in one piece this week. I spoke to the paperboy, like you said. He was fine about it.' He sounds relieved. 'His name's Logan. Must remember him when Christmas comes.' He pauses. 'Shall I get Susie up?'

Elspeth doesn't answer. Silence, floating and misty, muffles Susie's song and the grey, metallic, tinkling-clinking tune, driven by the disappearing string of the musical rabbit.

11

The Taxidermist

Monday

The doorbell rang and the dog went into a frenzy. 'Josh, I won't tell you again,' called Melissa as she passed the staircase on her way to the front door. It was always the last minute with Josh; his laid-back approach would drive her mad. He was such a contrast with Stella, his academic sister, who rose early and went to school without any nagging. Josh lingered in bed, half asleep among the chaos of discarded clothes, damp towels and dirty crockery, then zombie-like, akin to one of the creatures from the films he was so fond of, would lumber to the bathroom for his shower as if he had all the time in the world. Melissa had found warning notes from his guidance teacher in his school-bag, and he'd had detention a few times, but he remained steadfastly unhurried in the mornings, oblivious to the pace of the rest of the world. She didn't know who he took after. Her husband, Ian, was the most organised person in the world; he was the type who made up his lunch box the night before and always had a clean hankie.

A boy she hadn't seen before stood on the doorstep. He was wearing proper school uniform, unusual among Josh's friends, with an oversized thick quilted jacket, which was polished with a film of rain. 'Hi,' said Melissa. 'I'm afraid Josh isn't down yet. Do you just want to go on, or would you like to come in and wait.'

'I'll come in if that's all right, thanks,' said the boy.

Why had she asked? she wondered. 'Come in then, out the rain. Shut the door, will you, for the dog.' She moved toward the stairs and called again. 'Josh!' She turned to look at the boy. 'Sorry, what's your name?'

'I'm Ryan.'

'Josh. It's Ryan, 'she shouted. 'Hurry up.'

'Who?' called Josh from the landing.

Melissa smiled at the boy.

'It's my birthday tomorrow,' said Ryan. 'I'll be fourteen. I was held back a year. I get learning support in the base. I'm in S2.' His glasses had steamed up.

Melissa kept smiling. Most of Josh's friends were less forthcoming, and here she had a pithy biography of Ryan in a handful of words. It made her pleased that Josh seemed to have taken him under his wing. Pleased, but slightly surprised too. 'Happy birthday for tomorrow. Will you be doing anything special? Are you having a party?'

'No. I'm getting two Playstation games: The Last of Us and Doom Eternal. What's the dog called?' The family's Jack Russell had prised open the kitchen door after being shut in by Melissa and skittered over the floor tiles into the hall to check out the caller. His yapping turned to a gargle-like growl. He sniffed at Ryan's trousers, then wandered off dismissively.

'Pickles. Come on Pickles.' Melissa patted her thigh and bent down, calling Pickles to come over and meet Ryan properly.

Ryan stretched out a hand to pat it, but Pickles just growled.

'Pickles! Naughty boy. Get in your box,' said Melissa severely. 'Sorry Ryan. He's a bit old and grumpy.'

'I had a cat. Maybe he can smell it. She was called Linda, but she died. She was my only friend.'

'Oh, I'm sorry, Ryan,' said Melissa, her compassion swelling by the moment. Seemingly he didn't yet count Josh as a friend.

'Matthew and Connor at school call me "Brains". They call me "Brains" and go "doh doh doh" and laugh. But I don't mind. I like it in the base. That's the place you go if you need a bit of support, like me. We've been doing Anne Frank's diary. She was a girl in the Second World War who lived with her family in an attic behind a wardrobe hiding from the Nazis. She kept this diary and now we have to do the same, but I'm not very good with writing and I'm waiting for some help, but Mrs MacLean's busy just now.' Melissa nodded. She had an urge to wipe his glasses, but managed to control it. He was pale and his damp, black hair was almost in his eyes. It prompted her to sweep her own fringe back needlessly. 'A lot of what she wrote in the diary was just ordinary stuff which is funny when you think about what was going on outside the attic in the rest of the country. I can't remember where it was; Holland I think. At the end the diary just stops suddenly and I think they must have killed her. I expect they put her shoes and glasses on a big pile. That's what they did in those days. I don't know why they kept the stuff, but they did. There's going to be a school trip to go to the camp, but I won't be able to go on it. I'd like to see the stuff.'

Melissa wasn't sure how to respond. She put on her *wise* face. 'Yes, we're very lucky to live in these times,' she said.

At last Josh tumbled down the stairs in his usual dance-like fashion: step, step, pause; step, step, pause. 'Bye Ma!' He didn't have his tie on and the sleeves of his white shirt were rolled up. His fair hair had a rigid gelled quiff that looked as if it could take someone's eye out.

'What about your coat?'

'Nah, I'm fine.'

'And your breakfast?'

'I'll get something at the shop.'

He'd drive her mad. He passed Ryan with a grunt and headed through the door and down the path. Melissa supposed that good morning greetings between friends were no longer considered cool.

'Bye, Mrs Finnegan,' called Ryan, a few steps behind Josh.

She'd kept her maiden name, but didn't like to tell him. For a second she'd thought he was going to shake her hand. There was something old- fashioned about him. 'Bye, Ryan. Nice to meet you. Come again,' she added as he reached the gate.

Tuesday

Melissa was trying a different approach. Mothering Josh was not good for her mental well-being, she'd decided. She had taken up mindfulness, but needed to tackle the underlying cause. She went upstairs with a bacon sandwich and a mug of tea and put them beside his bed. 'Here you go Josh, rise and shine as Grandad used to say to me when I was little.' He groaned under his duvet and stirred a little. She opened the curtains. He just moaned at her. 'Need to get a move on,' she said. He moaned again.

The door bell rang and Pickles started up. She went down stairs, feeling agitated, and there was Ryan. 'Hello, Mrs Finnegan.'

'I'm sorry Ryan, Josh isn't even out of bed yet, you'd best just go on.'

'It's okay, Mrs Finnegan, I don't mind.' Pickles circled him, growling.

'Pickles, go in your box.' The dog went, hackles in a ridge along his back, but not before he was ready.

'It's my birthday today,' said Ryan.

'Oh, yes, of course. Happy Birthday Ryan. Did you get the games you wanted.'

'Yea, the Playstation's good because you can play it on your own. Mum says it's good cos it keeps me busy.'

'I'm hopeless at that kind of thing,' says Melissa. I had a go on one of Josh's games but I couldn't get on with it at all.'

'I try to make friends, but people call me names and laugh at me. Sometimes I can't help doing daft stuff. The other day I threw my school bag in the river. I don't know why, but someone told me to do it and I did and everyone had a laugh. I like it when people laugh at me, but the teachers say I shouldn't let them make fun of me. I couldn't live in an attic like Anne Frank if I didn't have any animals. I'd try to find a mouse to be friends with. There are lots of mice in old buildings. I'd give it some of my food. It would be better to be a bit hungry than not to have an animal. I've always liked animals. Sometimes I go into the pet shop just to smell the mice and other animals. I think it's a really nice smell. You can hold the rabbits and feel their knobbly backbones through their soft fur, and hold their hot ears between your fingers. But you can't lift them up by their ears because it hurts them. I've had lots of pets but they all die. I once found an injured pigeon and took it home to be my pet but it died. You can find frogs and newts if you know where to look. I like to cup them in my hand and feel them wriggling. Animals are good because you can look after them and they need you.'

'I've always liked the natural world,' said Melissa. 'Makes you feel better somehow.'

Josh came tumbling down the stairs. 'How was breakfast,' asked Melissa.

'Aye, good. Good plan. More tomato sauce next time.'

'It's Ryan's birthday today, Josh, did you know?'

'I thought you had a birthday last week?'

'That must have been somebody else,' said Ryan.

'Well, bye you two.'

Josh was already out of the door.

'Bye Mrs. Finnegan.'

'Just call me Melissa,' she said.

Wednesday

Melissa didn't like the idea of Josh having his breakfast in bed, but thought it might help to get him on the right shift. She took him a bowl of cornflakes and a mug of tea. She began peeling back his duvet, but he pulled it close to him. 'Oh, Josh, you don't have any pyjamas on.'

'Hmmm.' He squirmed about trying to get comfortable again. 'I was having such a nice dream. You're so cruel.'

Melissa gathered up some of the dirty crockery. She had thought if she left it long enough Josh would clear up himself, but that approach didn't seem to be working. A blue skin of mould had developed at the bottom of one of the mugs. She went downstairs and put it in the dishwasher. She'd have another go at him later. Didn't want to get the day off to a bad start. The door bell rang, the dog barked and there was Ryan on the doorstep. It was sunny and quite warm, but he still had his heavy coat on. 'Morning,' she said, 'I thought it would be you.' She gave him a smile. 'How was your birthday?'

'It was all right,' he said simply, while Pickles circled him with bared teeth.

Melissa picked up an envelope from the hall table and handed it to him. Inside was a card with a picture of a Barn Owl on the front. She'd written "best wishes on your birthday from Josh and Melissa". It wasn't exactly a birthday card but it was close. She hadn't told Josh.

'Sorry it's late. In your bed, you grumpy creature,' said Melissa. The dog reluctantly sloped off.

Ryan opened the card. 'Thank you,' he said. 'I'd like a dog but Mum says it would be too much trouble.

When I leave school I want to a taxidermist. I thought about being a vet, but you have to be good at science and I think being a taxidermist would be just as good. It would be like bringing dead animals back to life.   I saw a hedgehog the other day when I was on the bus. It was by the side of the road and I thought it was probably dead, but you never know, and it might have made a good pet, so when I got home I walked back along the road, it took me a while to get to where the hedgehog was, and I turned it over and there was a pink tube coming out of its stomach, like a big worm, and it was definitely dead. I put it in the hedge. You could see its teeth, like it was half smiling, half screaming, like it must have hurt when it died, so that shows it must have feelings. I touched the teeth. Its mouth was tight. I wondered about taking it home and stuffing it, but I didn't like the pink guts. I stuffed a bird once. It was a blackbird. I used soil and toilet paper, but Mum made me put it in the bin and said it was dirty.'

'There are some really good stuffed animals in the museum. Have you seen them? Very life-like.'

'We don't go into town. Mum says there are some funny people about.   In some ways it wouldn't be so bad being in an attic like Anne Frank, because you'd have people who'd have to be friends with you, but I don't like the ending. I'd have to change that and get away, jump off the train and hide in the forest on my own till the Americans came.'

Melissa was trying to think of something to say in response to this when Josh came tumbling down the stairs. The church clock was striking quarter to the hour. 'You're both going to be so late,' she said.

'It's fine,' said Josh. 'More sugar on the cornflakes next time, eh?'

'Bye Melissa.'

'Bye Ryan. Have a good day, both of you, she called.' Josh didn't look back, but she got a smile from Ryan.

Thursday

Melissa was trying the old vacuuming trick. She started on the landing, then naturally progressed to Josh's room, moving the clutter around, piling it on his chair and on the bed.

'Bloody hell,' he said, burying himself entirely under his duvet.

'Sorry, busy day ahead,' she lied, steering the Dyson around discarded socks and boxers. She was engrossed in her task when she saw a dark figure in the doorway and screamed. 'Oh, Ryan, I didn't see you there,' she said, recovering.

Josh's head emerged from his bedding. 'Bloody hell,' he said again. 'Can you all just get out of my f... flippin room.'

'I rang the bell,' said Ryan.

Melissa abandoned the vacuum and led the way down stairs. She'd shut Pickles in the kitchen and hadn't heard his barking above the sound of the cleaner.

'Josh doesn't like getting up, does he.'

'You could say that, Ryan. You seem to have no trouble.'

'I need to get Mum's breakfast ready before I go to school.'

Melissa was going to ask a follow up question, but Ryan carried on. 'Maybe I could take Pickles for a walk sometime?'

'He's a bit unpredictable. And I wouldn't like you to have to pick up the poo.'

Josh appeared, a bit sooner than expected. She turned to him. 'Josh, Ryan wondered if he might take Pickles for a walk one day. Maybe you could go with them?'

'Aye, that'll be right,' and he was out of the door with Ryan in his wake.

Friday

Josh was down before Melissa called him. The scent of aftershave clung to him. He had run Ian's razor over the downy covering of his cheek. 'What's happened to you?' she asked.

'What do you mean?'

'Well, look at you. You're up!'

'He's in love, Mum,' said Stella, who hadn't yet left the house. 'It's obvious. What a stink.'

'Are you, Josh? Are you in love?'

'I have to go,' he said.

'Is he? Is he in love?' she asked Stella.

'Mum, you are funny.'

Ryan didn't call that morning. Melissa missed him. **She** kept thinking about him during the day as she draped the washing over the clotheshorse and loaded the dishwasher and weeded the back garden. She thought about his dead cat, his interest in animals and his odd wish to be a taxidermist. She wondered about his life at home and his comment about having to get his mother's breakfast for her.

She asked Josh about him when he got home. Josh didn't know much. 'You shouldn't encourage him,' he said.

'What do you mean?'

'He's latched on to me and I haven't time. He's radge.'

'Everyone needs friends, Josh. Why don't you ask him round for tea one day? He seemed a bit sad to me.'

'Awa and bile yer heid.' Josh had been studying the Scots language at school.

Melissa told Ian about Ryan over a gin and tonic when he came in from work. 'You can't help everyone in the world,' he said.

'Oh, Ian. You don't mean that.'

'Best not to get involved. You know what you're like.'

It seemed providential, when, the next week, Melissa heard that her friend Vera's friend's cat had had kittens. Eight weeks old now and they were struggling to find homes for them. 'Such cute things,' said Vera. 'They're all black and white with cloudy blue eyes. I was tempted myself but Dennis would never have a cat. He's always leaping out into the garden to chase them away from the bird feeders. Did I tell you that he's taken to spraying the patio with his urine? He read somewhere that it deters them, but I haven't seen any sign of it yet.'

'Does he do that in the daylight?' asked Melissa.

Vera looked at her, then understood. 'He pees into a watering can in the shed,' she explained, laughing.

Melissa found out Ryan's address. The uncut grass in the front garden was turning to hay. There was a bicycle lying on its side, with grass growing through the spokes of the wheels. An old disused washing machine stood outside the door. Her knock was answered by a woman wearing a headscarf, a long black velvet dress and white evening gloves with soiled finger tips. She looked suspicious when she opened the door but then seemed really pleased when Melissa explained that she was the mother of one of Ryan's friends. She invited Melissa in. Two incense sticks were burning on the mantelpiece.

'What a lovely smell,' said Melissa, thought the scent was almost choking.

'Keeps away the evil spirits,' said Ryan's mother. 'You have to be so careful.'

Melissa laughed.

'What's funny?' asked Ryan's mum.

'Oh, nothing. No, I see', said Melissa.

Ryan's mum sat in an armchair, raised on wooden blocks, and offered Melissa a chair. She noticed Melissa looking at the blocks. 'The spirits can't pass through the wood,' she explained.

Melissa smiled, sympathetically. The chairs were all covered with Indian print throws and she had never seen as many scatter cushions.

Ryan's mother was enthusiastic about the idea of a new kitten. 'He'll be really pleased,' she said. 'He misses Linda so much. He doesn't have many friends. He's a good boy. I don't know what I'd do without him. He does all the shopping, you know?'

It was arranged that the kitten would be there for him when he got home from school next day. It was to be a surprise. Melissa would bring it round herself. She declined the offer of a cup of tea and headed home. Most of the houses and gardens were neglected and the roads were pitted with potholes. She passed a car, jacked up on bricks without any wheels and she jumped when a Rottweiler barked aggressively at her through a garden fence at the corner of the road.

She drove the kitten round the next day, in a wicker carrier she borrowed from Vera's friend. It mewed like a baby from its place on the passenger seat. 'It's all right,' Melissa kept saying, feeling the pain of the creature's separation from its mother. She gave Ryan's mother a few tins of cat-food to start them off. She watched as the mewing kitten was tipped from the carrier into a cardboard box, to await Ryan's return from school. 'I'm not a great fan of animals myself,' said Ryan's mother, who plainly didn't want to handle the kitten. Melissa gave her an uneasy smile, trying to hold back a coughing fit triggered by the rising spirals of incense.

Melissa shared her story with the family at teatime. Josh almost choked with incredulity. 'Did your friend, Ryan, tell you how his last cat died?'

'What do you mean?' asked Melissa uneasily. She was struck with the way Josh described Ryan as *her* friend.

'Word at school is that he dropped it out of the upstairs window, didn't he? To see if it really did have nine lives. Broke its neck of course.'

The rest of the family stopped eating, now that the story had become interesting.

'Oh, is that the boy in second year who was accused of crucifying those frogs?' asked Stella. 'Nailed them to a door, didn't he?'

'That's the one,' confirmed Josh.

Melissa opened her mouth to say something, then closed it again. 'Accused?' she said after a while. 'So nothing was proved.'

'I don't know. Who knows?' said Josh.

Melissa looked at her plate of food and thought of the little kitten she had delivered earlier, with its cloudy blue eyes. 'Maybe I should call round tomorrow?' she said, 'to see how they are all getting on.'

Melissa's husband, Ian, smiled unseen, as he put a piece of potato into his mouth.

Ten Years Later

'It's amazing.'

'How does he do it?'

'It's like it's alive, but in a freeze frame.'

Melissa and Ian looked at the Golden Eagle with a mixture of awe, fascination and pride. It had a dead rabbit in its claws and was looking defiantly at them as if it would turn on them if they made to touch its prey.

Later, at the graduation ceremony, Melissa could not hold back the tears when Ryan was awarded the Whittaker Prize for excellence in taxidermy. After the silver quaich was presented by the college principal Ryan turned to the audience in the hall. None of the other graduates had made speeches and Ian squirmed in his seat and wished he was somewhere else.

'I'd like to dedicate this prize to my late mum, who found life hard but was the bravest person in the world.' Ryan paused, and Ian breathed a sigh of relief, thinking it was all over. But it wasn't. 'And I'd like to thank Melissa and Ian for taking me in after Mum died, and Josh and Stella for putting up with me'.

There was a cry of 'You're my bro, Bro!' from the audience as Josh raised his hand with a thumbs up sign.

'Melissa always believed in me. She helped me to follow my dream and she's the reason I'm standing here today.' He stood there for a moment in the silence, then walked off to applause, punctuated by cheers from Josh and cries of 'Go Bro, go!'

12

Security

Lee leans right back, his arms ramrod straight, as he plunges into the forward sweep of the rushing swing, thrilling at the tilting trees against the summer sky, fathomless and blue as opals. The rushing air thrums in his ears. Then, as his feet reach the faltering height he thrusts his body forwards and bends his legs beneath him, and he falls back again, as the cracked asphalt spins in a blur below, till his body arcs backwards in readiness for the next dive. The rusting chains squeal against the crossbar as he dives and climbs, again and again, laughing to himself in his secret pleasure. But then, when his enjoyment is at its height, he notices the man, watching him from the old engine, half hidden behind its huge, flaking bulk.

Lee's joints jar as his trainers scrape against the crumbling grey ground and he brakes to a halt. He stands up and straightens his tie, his face reddening with the embarrassment of being discovered. The man comes out from behind the engine and they move towards each other. Lee looks around to see if anyone else is about. He runs a palm over his hair and flicks at some dirt on one of the navy button-down flaps of his military-style white shirt. The two men survey each other as the distance between them closes. Lee notices the man's soiled jacket and the stubble on his chin; neglect rather than designer. The man glances at the smiling ID picture of Lee, swinging on a lanyard, with the words, "Lee Scott, Security Guard" printed underneath.

'This is all private,' says Lee, with a sweep of his arm, 'I'm afraid you'll have to leave.'

'I was looking for Mr Henderson,' says the stranger.

'Who?'

'Mr Henderson: The headmaster.'

Lee smiles, just like his picture. 'There's only us here now,' he says. 'The security, I mean. They closed the school down about two years ago.'

'Yes, I see that now,' says the man. 'I've been wandering around the grounds. I didn't know they'd closed it down.'

The abandoned swing continues to squeak gently, as it rocks, ghost-like in the sunlight.

'I think they're going to turn it into luxury flats,' Lee tells him.

'Is that right? I was here, you see, when it was a school. I was in the area and I thought I'd call in. I'd like to have seen Mr Henderson. You don't know where I can find him, I suppose?'

'No, sorry,' says Lee, 'but I've seen his name on some stuff.'   There are some files in a damp, unlit walk-in cupboard in the basement. Sometimes, to pass the time during the long shifts, Lee has pried between their flimsy, buff coloured cardboard covers under the yellow light of his torch. They are mostly a jumble of carbon-copy sheets of tissue-like paper, held together by treasury tags. The typing is blue and slightly blurred; shards of lives written in the age of manual typewriters and correction-fluid, many of them put together before Lee was born. They smell of dampness and of the people who handled them; dispersed and disconnected now from the bonds which once tied them together so closely in the community of the school. Mr Henderson's signature appears in lots of them, written in a fountain pen with blue ink.

The man looks over towards the main building. 'Everything looks so much smaller,' he says, 'even the loco.'

They turn towards the shell of the ancient railway engine, set on the edge of the play area, grass and bindweed pulling and twisting among its rusted wheels.

'How the hell did they get that thing up here?' asks Lee, who has often wondered.

'God knows. It's always been there. I never thought about it really.'

Lee's got a friendly nature. It's hard to see how he'd confront a violent intruder.   'Looks like a great place for kids?' he says.

The man reaches inside his jacket pocket and draws out a packet of cigarettes. Lee accepts the offer of one and strikes a match, the flame from which they share behind cupped hands. 'Trying to give up really,' says Lee.

The man smiles. 'Life's too short,' he says.   The comment could be taken either way.

They both look across to the main building, fifty yards away. A portico with a Grecian frieze leans upon Doric columns, which front massive doors, reached by a sweep of steps, but sealed now.   Years ago liveried servants would have stood there, welcoming their master's return.   Now an expansive, smothering growth of clematis creeps upwards and inwards, its flowers withering, as its tendrils claim the edges of the steps and feel their way up the columns, like a fragment of jungle reclaiming a long-abandoned temple.

'It's amazing how quickly these old places begin to fall apart, once they're empty,' says Lee, speaking like an expert.   'The roof's leaking and there are pigeons nesting in one of the rooms upstairs; crap everywhere. And there's still lots of stuff lying about.   It's funny, cos although no-one touches it, it just seems to get messier by itself.   It looks as if they left in a hurry; there are boxes of files in one of the cupboards, and even some stuff still written up on the blackboards in the classrooms. I suppose once everyone knew the place was going to close nobody cared about it any more.'

The man's forehead is peppered with beads of sweat. Lee wonders why he's wearing his jacket. It's a cheap version of the heavy waxed sort; must be hot.

'Where'd you leave your car?' asks Lee.

'Eh?' He's in a reverie. Stirring white-scarred memories; uncorking bottled up recollections. He re-focusses on Lee. 'No. I came on the bus. I walked up from the village.' He draws on his cigarette and the smoke sputters out of his mouth in staccato puffs as he speaks. 'I like walking. I once walked the whole of the Pennine Way. I started off with just an old sleeping bag and an apple. Two hundred and sixty eight miles. And when I got to the end I turned round and walked all the way back again. Scrounged food. Vicarages are good for that stuff.' He pinches out the end of his cigarette between his finger and thumb and puts the stub in his pocket for later. 'Anyway, I'd better be off now. I just wanted a look, and to see if I could find Mr Henderson.'

Lee pulls at his own cigarette then stubs it out on the gravel. The man looks at the shredded remains. 'Why don't you come in for a mug of tea, now you're here,' Lee asks him. You could have a quick look round. Seems a shame to have a wasted journey.'

So it's settled, and Lee leads the way through a side door and into the shadow-filled passages, so gloomy in contrast to the white sunshine outside that they have to put out their hands to feel their way along the angular twists and turns, until their eyes adjust. They pass through the large main hall, silent and church-like behind the now sealed front doors. An ugly hole, fringed with rubble disfigures one of the walls, and around it crumbling masonry and plaster have become trodden into the once gleaming wooden floors, which used to be buffed each day by a cleaner with a monstrous vibrating machine, the sound of which still reaches sometimes into the man's dreams.

'They didn't have Security at first,' explains Lee, 'but a few things got nicked so they brought us in. It was a good fireplace I think.'

'It had carved leaves and flowers along the top. The boys used to chip them off when no-one was looking. It was a kind of dare. We were all vandals.'

'This way,' says Lee and leads him to the little room the security firm has claimed as its office. He boils a kettle and makes tea in two stained mugs, using a spoon to squeeze the teabags against the insides of the mugs before flinging them into a nearby metal bin. While he's waiting the man bends to look at a photograph that is stuck to the wall above the desk.

'That's my girlfriend with our baby, Marc. Course, he's bigger now; nearly three months'.

'You're a lucky man,' says the man.

Lee smiles proudly. Marc hadn't been planned, but he's the best thing that's ever happened to Lee. He couldn't hold back the tears when he first held him against his cheek in the hospital, just minutes old, his blue eyes roving in the new light as Lee held him safe. He'd brought Kate to see the place where he worked when she was heavily pregnant, and they'd stood beneath the cherry trees, which had radiated light and hummed with the song of bees. The blossom had snowed fluttering petals down upon them, while Lee held his palm on Kate's belly and felt the baby kick.

'This was Mr Moody's room,' says the man. 'He was Head of Care. He used to wear a tweed jacket and smoke a pipe. He always seemed to be putting it into his pocket while it was still alight. We hoped he'd catch fire, but he never did. He liked doing crosswords. We assumed it was part of his official duties. It's funny what comes back to you after all these years.' He looks into the middle-distance of the past, stirring up memories like piles of brown dried-out leaves, layers covering each other, from years ago. He sips his tea, and Lee notices his bitten down fingernails.

'How long ago is it?'

'Twenty-eight and a half years.'

After they finish their tea the man leads them on a tour. They've both seen it all before, but not like this. In the enormous dining hall steel shutters close off the serving hatches, throwing back cloudy images of the two figures. The man goes through a side door into the kitchen beyond. 'I never came back here before. It was good food, I'll say that.'

In the recreation room there's still a ping-pong table at one end. The man strokes it with his fingertips, trailing waves of dark furrows across the dusty green surface. A corner of the room is cordoned off by half glazed partitions. 'So they could keep an eye on us,' he explains. 'This was the TV area.' The shelf from which the television used to throw its images onto the upturned faces is still screwed in place, high up in a corner.

*

There are fragments in the files:

...Michael Roberts had to be restrained again last night. He lost control of himself completely after evening meal and lashed out at Harold Scully for no reason. Removed his shoes and locked him in his room...

*

As they go up the main staircase, each of them twists his palm on the mahogany pineapple newel on the banister, the way countless numbers have done before them, including the man himself when he was inside the skin of the frightened boy he had once been. A carved wooden sailing ship lies beached in a fallen cloud of dead flies and dust on a windowsill at the turn; light from the blue stained panes washes over it like a powdery sea.

'Mr Brown was Woodwork,' says the man, nodding towards the ship..

'Must've taken hours,' says Lee.

'After my time, I think.'

*

...Sean shows an aptitude for woodwork, but today for no apparent reason he used a claw-hammer to smash up the pencil case he had been making. He was in tears afterwards but would not talk about it...

*

They reach the top of the stairs and make their way along various corridors. 'This was the room I slept in,' says the man. 'There were seven of us in here, and some nights we all wet the bed. I can still remember the smell of urine in the mornings.' He stands in the centre of the room, feeling like the powerless child once more, trapped in a little world that had its own rulers, laws and rituals.

Lee sniffs the air. He crosses the room to the bay window. The man joins him, and together they look down the avenue of cherry trees to the distant hills beyond. 'I used to think about running away, but I never did. No-where to go. They always brought you back anyway.'

*

...Eight boys absconded last night and had to be returned by the police at two a.m. Home leave for all eight to be cancelled for the next four weeks. There was a full moon and I am convinced there is a connection...   D Henderson

*

He faces the centre of the room again. 'We'd have to pile the wet sheets and pyjamas in the middle of the room and tie them together in a big bundle ready for the laundry. Then we'd all have to have a shower. They shouted at you if you tried to hide yourself. There was one guy who used to scream the place down. They tried coaxing him, and when that didn't work they'd sometimes use force. He'd just scream and scream. He wasn't right in the head, that one. Got moved eventually.'

'Why were you here? Had you been in trouble or something?' asks Lee.

The man is silent for a moment. 'I don't know,' he says. 'Nobody ever really explained. I wasn't very good at school, and things weren't easy at home, but I don't know why they sent me here exactly.'

*

...Dear Jim,

Just a few lines hoping to find you well, as we are here. It was nice to get your letter last week. We miss you and all, but if you stick in they might let you come home for a weekend soon. I can't come and see you just now because it's too far, but Mary's got a new boyfriend, and he's got a car, so maybe he'll bring us up sometime. The weather hasn't been too good lately, lots of rain. We've had to get rid of your rabbit as I just couldn't do with the cleaning out. Dad goes in for another operation soon. Work hard son and behave yourself.

Love Mam...

*

Lee whistles a tune in the empty silence. It echoes briefly around the room, then dies in the stale air. They go back downstairs and into a classroom. 'They've taken the desks away,' observes the man, disappointedly. 'I used to sit about here.' He stands in the place. Some numbers are chalked up on the blackboard and in one corner there is a drawing of an erect penis. Lee's seen it before, and sniggers when the man notices it. But he blushes and turns away when the man rubs it out with the side of his hand, leaving a greasy smudge. It seems to be the cue to end the tour.

Back outside the sunshine is dazzling.

'Thanks,' says the man.

'No problem. Trip down memory lane, eh?'

They shake hands and Lee watches the man as he walks away along the avenue of cherry trees. Once he disappears round a bend in the drive Lee goes back to his office and at the sight of Marc's photo impulsively sends a message of love to Kate. Hidden behind a screen of overgrown laurels the man has turned for one last look. He wonders if Mr Henderson is still alive, and if he knows anything. About how he used to be taken off to one of the housefather's rooms at night for a game of draughts, or to watch a TV programme, with chocolate biscuits and Coke. It had been good, just to be away from the constant noise of living in a crowd, and it had seemed natural when Mr James had taken off his shirt and drunk beer in just his trousers. Then, later, the touching had started. At first it had been a laugh between them, till he became trapped in the secrecy of it all. 'This is our secret, okay?' And he hadn't been able to tell anyone: not then, nor since. He wonders how many staff? How many boys? Or was it just him?

*

The fire had got a fatal hold by the time the fire engines arrived from the nearest station, over twenty miles away. The orange glow from the blaze could be seen from three counties, and the fire fighters could do nothing but wait and make a gesture with their hoses. Inside, the model boat, the ping-pong table and the pineapple newel turned to ash, and the floors collapsed and the roof gave way amid tremendous crashing and roaring. Once the fire had died down the building had to be demolished because it was so unstable. There were rumours about it all being a set up for the insurance, but then Lee was arrested and months later he was found guilty of arson after a trail. Afterwards it transpired that he'd had a number of previous convictions in his youth, including one for fire-raising. He protested his innocence, and described a man who had visited on the day of the fire, but the police could find no leads to follow. It had been discovered that Lee had bought a can of petrol the day before, and the remains of a can was found in the rubble. There was footage of Lee in the forecourt of a filling station. Lee said he'd bought the petrol to cut the grass at home. There was a can of petrol in his garden shed, but the jury's verdict was unanimous.

Kate stopped visiting Lee after the first few weeks of his sentence. She told him that it wasn't that she didn't believe him, but Marc became sick during the long bus journey, and she didn't think prison visits were good for him.

13

Gold

The fish tank had been lying in a corner of the garage since Olivia had left. I'd emptied it of course, except for the gravel, which had dried out. The glass was streaked with brown stains. I cleaned it in the kitchen and carried it up to Olivia's bedroom, which was just as she'd left it; we'd always hoped she would come back one day; would get in touch, would tell us she was alive at least. Her posters of aggressive rock bands were still on the walls, along with her certificate for winning the school poetry prize and a print of Salvador Dali's *Metamorphosis of Narcissus*; the exploratory journey of the teenager. Siobhan cleaned the room every week; she would open drawers and touch the few clothes that Olivia hadn't taken away. And every week she asked me if I thought Olivia was still alive. 'Of course,' I'd say. But we'd both lie awake at night. And I would have to whisper, 'it's all right, it's all right,' stroking her arm when Siobhan had nightmares. It had been two years. We thought about her every stretching day; every aching hour. Our brains were numb, like when a foot goes to sleep after you have sat with your legs crossed for too long. But maybe that was better than the needles and pins that can follow.

I moved to and from the bathroom with buckets of water to fill the fish-tank which I'd put on the little table where it used to stand. I connected the electric water filter and put the lid on, Siobhan watching from the door. The water began swirling, murky from the dusty gravel, lit up by the little strip light in the lid. Siobhan said she was amazed it all worked, but I knew it would. I knew everything was going to be all right now. I buried the plant roots in the gravel and put the fish into the tank, still floating in their plastic bags. I'd bought three little goldfish and some plants from the out of town shopping store on my way home from work.

Siobhan fetched a cloth from the bathroom and dabbed at the spotted trail of water I'd left. 'I can't believe she's coming home,' she said. 'I won't believe it till she's really here.' She began crying and I gave her a hug.

'Tomorrow,' I said. 'She'll be here tomorrow night.'

Later we had our tea on our knees in front of the TV, though neither of us took much in. Afterwards I went up to check on the tank. The water was beginning to clear. I scraped the inside of the glass with an old plastic loyalty card and turned the fish loose. I half expected them to turn belly-up immediately, but they seemed fine.

'Why?' Asked Siobhan. 'Why the fish?' She was beside me, bending over to look at them.

'I don't know. I can't explain it,' I said. 'I just had to do it. Stupid.'

'No, it's a lovely thing to do,' said Siobhan. 'A special welcome home present.'

When we went to bed I read the notes I'd been given with the fish. They gave advice about letting the water stand for several days before adding plants, and then leaving the tank to get established before introducing any fish. At around three in the morning I went through to have a look at them and switched on the aquarium light. They seemed happy enough and the water was becoming less cloudy.

The fish-tank had originally been a birthday gift to Olivia a few years back. It had felt even then like she was slipping away from us. She'd changed from the little girl who'd worn flouncy dresses and performed party pieces on her violin, to someone who seemed to hate everything we said and did. She came home with love bites on her neck and the odour of cigarettes clinging to her leather jacket. She accentuated her anger with dark eye make-up, and, when she was home at all she stayed in her room. She stopped trying at school; she skived off during the day. Such a waste, the teachers said. They expected us to sort her out. It had been a stupid present. 'What would you like for your birthday?' I'd asked, as brightly as I could. She'd always liked presents, and even then had smiled at the thought of a gift. 'Give me a surprise,' she'd challenged.

Something to care for, I'd thought. Something to bring her out of herself. Siobhan knew better. 'We'll get her an Ipad as well,' she'd said.

I'd wrapped the aquarium up in girly birthday paper; it had taken three sheets. I thought she'd find it funny. But she was *so* disappointed. She didn't even take the aquarium out of its box. But she liked the Ipad. I'd tried to explain. Told her she'd always liked animals and I reminded her of a trip to the Sea Life Centre some time back. 'Do you remember how lovely you thought the fish were?' But she didn't want to remember.

The fish-tank had remained in its box for weeks. Then I suggested setting it up in her bedroom. She agreed, but just to keep me quiet. 'How about coming with me to choose some plants?' I'd suggested. We went into town and called at one of those old fashioned pet shops. There was just a glimmer of enthusiasm. She chose a couple of rocks and a "No fishing" sign to be lodged in the gravel in amongst the plants. But she didn't come home with me and we'd sat up till 2 a.m. waiting for her key in the door.

Over the next few weeks I had populated the tank with a few guppies, a couple of zebra fish and a few black mollies; back in those days the fish-tank was heated. She pretended not to be interested, but a couple of times I caught her watching them intently, and once I found her talking to them, though I couldn't hear what she said. After she reached sixteen she came home less and less often. We had arguments. We told her she was breaking our hearts. We said we loved her. We asked what her grandparents would have thought, trying to reach a sense of guilt that might pull her back. We pleaded. We wept. We locked her in her room, but she climbed out of the window. I don't know how she didn't break her neck. We confronted her about drugs and drink. She lied to us all the time. Eventually we accepted defeat; we couldn't go on like this. She moved out. I shifted some of her things for her and Siobhan bought her sets of sheets and towels. She didn't know whether to get single sheets or doubles – it was comical looking back. In the end she got doubles – she could always fold them over. It was a dingy flat in town, with dirty washing-up in the sink, grime everywhere and a filthy carpet. I gave the scum-lined washbasin a quick clean when I went to the bathroom to relieve myself. When I came out she was in the arms of a lad who had no shirt on. They separated when I coughed in the doorway.

'I'll be off then, love,' I'd said after a few moments. 'Now, is there anything you need?'

Olivia had followed me to the door. 'No, Dad, I'll be fine. It's what I want. I've got to have some space.' She was like a caricature; a character in a soap.

'Give me a phone. Anytime. Do you hear?' I'd bent over and kissed her cold cheek. 'Is he your boyfriend?' I'd whispered.

'Oh, Dad', she'd said.

After that she occasionally came home at the weekends. She said she'd got a job in a shop, but we still gave her money. Siobhan used to try and fill her up with decent food, but she'd become very picky; suspicious almost of anything that we thought might be good for her. She told us nothing. We tried so hard not to fall out, but you just can't watch and say nothing, can you?

'You will tell us if there's anything wrong, won't you?'

'I'm fine. Stop worrying.'

One time she'd bent over to look at the fish. 'One of the guppies has died,' she'd said, seeing me in the doorway. It had sunk to the bottom and its eyes had turned white. A loach was pecking away at its torn flank. Later I'd hooked it out with the little green mesh net and chucked it towards the flowerbed; the final resting-place of all the fish that had died. Then one day she came and the tank was empty. The last fish had died, so I'd switched off the pump and the plants too had slowly died. It had gone out of my mind. She tapped the glass, but nothing stirred. She stood there for ages, just looking at the still, dead water through the green, slime-covered glass. It was then that I took it to the shed.

That was the last time we saw her. I went round to her flat but she'd moved. We occasionally got a text; she'd reply to about one in ten. They said very little, but Siobhan would read them over and over. 'I'm fine. Wrking n another shop now. C u sum time.' It was reassuring to hear something of her. We always put lots of X's on our texts, but she never did on hers. Then it all stopped. Her phone didn't seem to be working. I tried her old friends but not one of them could tell me anything. I'd go into town and drive around the streets at night. Nothing. We kept putting money into her bank account, but didn't know if she got it. We contacted the police but they weren't interested. Happens all the time, they said. We advertised in the Big Issue. Not a sign. We got angry. How could she leave us worrying like this? We got frantic. Someone's taken her. She must be dead. It was a living nightmare. And friends and family had to know. How do you explain it? Their look seemed to say it was our fault; we must have done something. Our little Olivia who used to play her violin for them all as a party piece. Who'd won the school poetry prize. Weeks, months, a year...

Then out of the blue, she phoned. 'Hi Dad. I need to come home for a while. I'll see you the day after tomorrow.'

'Olivia! Olivia! God, it's so good to hear your voice. We've been frantic. Siobhan, it's Olivia. Are you okay? Do you want me to come and get you?'

'No, it's fine. Archie will bring me.'

'Who?'

'It doesn't' matter. I'll see you soon, okay?'

I took the day off work. 'Thank God, she's coming home,' I said. Siobhan cleaned the house from top to bottom and I weeded the garden. Siobhan cooked a chicken curry; always one of Olivia's favourites. We paced about; waiting, wondering. Time passed, so slowly. Maybe she wouldn't come home after all. Maybe she'd changed her mind. Siobhan plumped up the cushions and moved the photos on the mantelpiece by a fraction: a family portrait; Olivia's first day at school; Olivia on a pony.

She walked in as if she'd never been away. She still had a key and we went into the hall when we heard it in the door. She'd come by taxi. So much for Archie, whoever he was. There was a pile of stuff on the doorstep; suitcases, bin liners bulging with things, and a baby's buggy... And there she was, at last, in the hall, home. 'Hi Dad. Mum. This is Zack.' The baby was in a sling around her neck; his head resting against her, his eyes tightly closed, his head wrapped in a little woolly hat. She took him out carefully and gently handed him to Siobhan, who cradled him in her arms, smiling down into his little turning face, everything kaleidoscopic through her tears. I bent over and stroked the baby's cheek with my finger. He grasped my pinkie. He couldn't be more than a few days old. 'He looks just like you,' I said. 'When you were a baby.'

Later, we all went upstairs and set up the moses basket in Olivia's room. 'It's good to be home,' she said, looking round. She took off her leather jacket and slung it over the back of a chair. Then she noticed the aquarium. The waters had cleared and the goldfish shone under the lights through the crystal clear glass. 'But they're so beautiful,' said Olivia. She bent down to look more closely. The fish rose, expecting to be fed, and she scattered some flakes of fish-food on the surface. She held Zak up to have a look. 'Look, Zak, look at the little fishes; little creatures of pure gold, just for you.' She held him next to her cheek and we all bent down to watch the fish.

14

Three For a Girl

The bus swings into the stop and the heads of the passengers sway in perfect choreography. An empty coke can ricochets off human feet and chrome seat legs. Fragments of conversations briefly become distinct, then fall silent as the driver kills the engine, throws open his cab door and heaves himself into the aisle. He's a big man and has to sidestep his way to the rear, touching seat-backs and breathing heavily. His raised finger jabs the air as he gets closer to the boys; his turned-up shirt-cuffs falling back to expose tattoos, indistinct among a thick covering of arm hair.

'Any more trouble and you'll be off, do you hear?' He casts a threatening shadow over the boys, blocking out the slanting sunlight and dousing the drifting dust motes. 'I'd soon sort you out if you was mine, I can tell you.'

There are a few murmurs of approval. He turns to Barbara, who is sitting a couple of rows in front of the boys.

'Okay, love?' He bends over her and gently picks some paper pellets out of her hair. She submits meekly, just as she had submitted while the boys had flicked their missiles towards her. 'Come and sit near the front, so I can keep an eye on you,' says the driver.

Earlier, the smooth, silky wrapping-paper had crackled like wafers of ice between Barbara's fingers as she'd pressed it against the softness inside. The sticky-tape had squealed like a pierced animal when she'd pulled it from its roll before snipping through it with the scissors. The cruel slicing noise warned that they could shear through flesh: could sever an artery or cut an umbilical cord. She'd left the scissors lying on the carpet, which, unusually for her, she hadn't vacuumed for hours. Her reflection had quivered in the mirrored edges, so she'd thrown a cushion over them. Barbara spends a lot of her time cleaning the house; a bit like Lady Macbeth trying to get rid of that spot; trying to expunge her sense of guilt.

She'd bought a card too. The two women behind the cash desk seemed to whisper knowingly, as if they could see her frozen memory of Jessica, in the pretty pink Babygro with a satin rabbit motif, her face discoloured by bruises and her dead eyes half open on a world she'd never known. The card had an embossed pink rabbit on the front, with large, Bambi eyes. Afterwards she'd doubted her choice, but it was too late.

2 Today. Happy Birthday to a Special Girl!

Inside she'd written: "To my darling daughter, Jessica. With all my love, Mummy." She'd put two kisses at first, one for each year, but it hadn't felt enough, so she'd put twenty-four, one for each month, before licking the gum and sticking down the flap. The bad taste had lingered on her tongue all morning.

She and the driver catch each other's reflections in his mirror, shining in the spinning light. She presses the bell and the bus pulls in to a stop next to the crematorium.

'Orright, love?' he calls, as she steps down through the double doors in the centre.

Her head is down and she gives no sign. The doors close behind her with a sigh, and the whining bus pulls into the stream of traffic, which has to slow and give way. The receding boys bare their teeth and give her the fingers through the back window.

She goes through the black, forbidding iron gates, which lean over her like cold shadows, and she follows the lonely winding path through the trees; their fresh, unsullied spring leaves unfurling to the sunlight for the first time.

They'd all said it was the perfect time of year to have a baby, with spring and summer stretching before them. They'd painted the little bedroom a gender-neutral yellow; they didn't want to know if it was going to be a boy or a girl. The cot was bought, her mother had crocheted blankets, the pram was ready; everything was in place. When she was pregnant she'd pictured herself and Derek picnicking in the park, he holding their baby aloft against high, white rolling clouds and blue skies.

A couple of laughing magpies flash black against white amongst the trees and shrubs. They bounce across the grass, feet together, full of confidence and a sense of importance. One for sorrow, two for joy. They'll pull the entrails from a dead rabbit if they find one.

Jessica's two today, but she'll always be a baby. There's something nice about that, Barbara thinks. Everybody loves babies: they haven't had time to hurt anyone. The birthday present is in her bag, along with a cake. 'Some lucky little girl,' the smiling assistant had said. She seemed nice, Barbara thought. Her checkout made a bleeping noise as she scanned the cake through. 'Here, let me put it in a carrier for you. We had one just like this for my granddaughter's birthday. It was delicious.' The folds of her nylon overall had hissed and stirred as she worked.

Once home the icing had cracked as she'd pushed two little pink candles with spiralling white candy stripes into the perfect surface. The candles were in plastic holders of pirouetting ballerinas. She'd lit them and each ballerina had held their weeping torch aloft, the flames trembling in the darkened room behind the drawn curtains, while the brilliant sunlight edged them in a searching aura. She'd stared at them burning down, dribbling wax onto the cake till they died away to leave her alone.

There's a funeral taking place in the chapel and the car park is overflowing, with beached cars leaning on the grass verges, blocking each other in at angles, as if in silent, fish-eyed conversations. She passes through a group of mourners who have lingered after an earlier funeral, stepping out of life's slipstream into the curious world of sanitised death. Some of the men have earrings and cropped hair and they smoke, holding their cigarettes down against their sides between sucks and checking their phones. A woman in a bright red coat gives her a smile and she looks away. A few people are crying. The chapel is like a departure lounge, and whoever it is they have come to see off has been taken behind the curtains, but they seem reluctant to leave.

Barbara enters the chapel on impulse and a few heads turn to look; another service has started; there is a tight schedule. A minister is talking about a man called Tony, cut down before his time. The chapel is full to bursting; so different from little Jessica's funeral. She wants to share their grief and to share her grief with them, but she drops her umbrella, and it makes a clattering noise on the flagstones. Heads twist around to look at her and she gathers herself together and leaves, trying to be quiet. As she walks away, back in the bright daylight, she imagines the service going on inside the chapel; all those people, remembering, exchanging comfort. There had only been five people at Jessica's funeral. Her mother had thought it odd to have a funeral at all, as if Jessica hadn't been a real person.

In the garden of rest Barbara can still hear the magpies clack and cackle, way over across the undulating landscaped grounds. A ragged carrier bag has caught on a rose bush and it whispers in the breeze, which tugs and tightens it. She looks around, but there is no-one to do anything.

She knows exactly where to find the name on the redbrick wall:

In Loving Memory of Jessica.

She touches the little brass plate with a kiss she puts on her fingers. She wishes Jessica had been buried; that there was a place that held her in the earth. After they had tipped her ashes over the soil it had felt like they'd thrown her away. She'd instinctively bent to catch what was really just a puff of dust, but Derek had pulled her back, and held her hand tightly as if she was a child.

There had been too many people in the birthing room and she'd known something was wrong, but surely no-one had stillbirths these days? Derek hadn't been able to bring himself to take her outstretched hand. Later, she'd felt nothing as she lay among the starched white linen, crumpled by her struggle, surrounded by the useless technology that had bleeped and flashed as Jessica had been born then died moments afterwards. She'd lain in the ward alongside other new mothers; their babies beside them in transparent plastic cots, watching their visitors come and go with gifts and kisses, while she waited alone until the doctor could find time to see her and tell her she could leave. All she had was a photograph of Jessica on her phone, in her pink Babygro. She had to keep it secret from Derek so he wouldn't delete it.

She tiptoes across the rose bed, her shoes sinking into the soft soil. The barbs of the rose bushes catch her stockings and scratch her legs, but she pushes on till she reaches the carrier bag and tears it from the rose bush. Then it's time to go. As she walks back to the entrance to the crematorium she's drawn to a bench among the trees. She reads the little brass plate screwed into its back.

In fondest memory of Effie

Dear mother, grandmother and
great-grandmother.

Died 2017, aged 93.

She sits down on the bench, takes out the birthday cake and offers a piece to the grey squirrels which undulate lightly across the grass, their plumed tails held out behind, but they're not interested. She breaks off some more, but it too lies untouched on the close-clipped grass. She puts a shard of icing into her mouth, but it's too sweet and it makes her feel sick. She quickly mashes up the rest of the cake, scatters it over the grass, and moves on. After a while she looks back to see the magpies hopping and strutting over the grass, croaking in rasping voices and stabbing at the cake with their dark, shining beaks. There are three of them: three for a girl.

Barbara decides to walk home rather than take the bus. She passes a terrace of handsome Victorian houses and sees a pram in the small front garden of one. The gate is open and she goes into the garden and leans over to look inside the pram. The baby is asleep, her eyelids flickering and her lips sucking at the air. Barbara reaches into her bag for Jessica's present, which she thinks she might leave for the baby, but then she has a better idea. She lets off the pram's brake, and pushes the sleeping baby away; it's the most natural thing in the world. Passers-by smile at her as she wheels the baby along the street. With each step she grows taller; she was born to be a mother. Back home she unwraps the present, and the paper falls to the floor, white-side up, like a huge distorted eggshell. Inside is a cuddly cat with a bow round its neck. 'Here you are Jessica,' she says. 'Look what I've got for you.' She has propped up the baby in a corner of the sofa, but she just cries and cries and pushes the toy away when Barbara offers it to her. Barbara goes upstairs to Jessica's room and finds a little dress from within the piles of folded, unworn baby clothes that lie in the chest of drawers. She takes it downstairs and lays it beside the baby. It's far too small; it's very disappointing. She looks at her watch and gets to her feet. 'Daddy'll be home shortly,' she says, 'I must get on with the vacuuming.'

15

Not Ready For Love

Teenagers have been drawn to the area outside Mario's fish and chip shop for years. They share the odd poke of chips, smothered in sauce, but gather mainly for the banter, the visual warmth of the light spilling into the otherwise empty night-time street and the comforting smells of frying fish, warm pizzas and hot Scotch pies. There isn't much else to do; the youth club isn't for them and bus trips into town are beyond the reach of most. The camaraderie of the group and the dramas that arise from nothing much provide a powerful magnet. Customers thread their way through the little group, twisting their shoulders and shuffling sideways like shore crabs to get inside. Everyone knows everyone and the knot of young people on the pavement has been there for as long as anyone can remember, though its membership changes. Greetings are periodically exchanged between arriving customers and the social gathering outside. 'Hi Zoe, how're you doing?' It's Mrs Graham, an English teacher from the school. 'Oh great, thanks,' replies Zoe, slightly pink and self-conscious. The group talks mostly together in low tones, sharing the odd smoke and having a laugh. They will move to the pavilion in the park later for a few cans. It is something of an exclusive club and not everyone is welcome.

It's a dark, drizzly Friday night, but not wet enough to drive them away. 'Oh, Christ, look who's coming,' says the Hulk. They all look round and some scowl and snigger in derision, as Bingy comes on towards them. He is not a member of the club. He is swaying slightly from side to side; he's been drinking cans in the hollowed out holly bush down by the river with his pals, Gazz and Spike. He'd wanted them to come to the chippy with him, but they know their place, so he'd come alone. They said they might see him later. Bingy is in love with Zoe. He's an old romantic and he's got it bad. She has long blond hair, perfect skin, lips that make him salivate when he looks at them and she wears her school uniform like no-one else: short, tight skirt, loose tie, breasts pushing against her blouse, though he tries not to think too much about that because his love is pure. He's always on the lookout for her. He waits for her on the corner behind a tree near her house on the off chance of just glimpsing her as she comes and goes. It's out of his way, but he takes the same route to school as she does, treading the path she has walked, just in case of a sighting. He sleeps with a used tissue she'd dropped under his pillow. When, very occasionally, they come face to face, he always says the wrong thing; something pathetic like, 'shame about the rain', or 'only two days before the weekend' or 'I'm getting a new phone.' She sometimes smiles. Afterwards he blushes as he goes over and over what he's said and laments the lost opportunities. Zoe is kind to him and usually makes some bland response. He's texted her and messaged her and sent her funny film clips of cute animals falling over, with laughing Emogis, but she never responds. In fact she's blocked him. But still she is kind when they come face to face, so he lives in hope. Love is tortuous. He is mystified by it but he clings to hope. So he decided to go past Mario's just to see if Zoe is there, just to be near her and get a fix of her beauty.

Zoe *is* there. She's there with the Hulk, though nobody calls him that to his face. He plays rugby and is in love with his body; his bedroom smells of deodorant and is full of weights, and mirrors, so he can watch his muscles tighten as he does his exercises. Bingy thinks Zoe should have better taste. He aches inside with his love for her. He wishes he was a bit more confident; his gran is always telling him he needs to put himself forward a bit more. 'You're a good looking lad, Richard,' she says to him, 'as good as any of them.' She always calls him Richard. And she'll look at the photo of her long-dead husband on the mantelpiece. 'Your granda was a fine looking man, God rest his soul, and you're just like him.'

But you can't force yourself to be something you're not. Bingy's gran worries about everything, especially after all that happened to Bingy's mum. But that's another story. Tonight, there is Zoe with the Hulk. There's a bit of a crowd, and they've got a few cans in carrier bags for later and one or two are smoking. There's some tinny music coming from a phone somewhere. A police car has just driven slowly by and they've exchanged nods with the officers inside. Bingy positions himself on the edges of the group and pretends to busy himself with his phone; scrolling down meaningless information, not taking any of it in. No-one bothers much about him; he's not one of them, but he's harmless. He tries not to look at Zoe, but then his heart jumps as he sees that the Hulk has his hand on her buttocks and is sucking away at her face with his tongue half way down her throat. Bingy can't bear it; it's torture, but he can't stop looking. Then he sees her try to pull away. He tenses up. The rest of the group have respectfully turned their heads to the street, but Bingy sees what's happening. It's agonising. The Hulk glares at him. 'What you looking at, eh?' and Bingy turns away without saying anything. But then he thinks he hears Zoe say, 'Stop it Finn.' That's the Hulk's real name. 'No, stop it,' she says. Bingy is sure that's what she says, and she kind of stumbles and her eyes meet Bingy's, just for a second, and in that second Bingy rises like a hero. 'Leave her alone, Finn,' he says. It just comes out; he hadn't planned it at all. The Hulk detaches himself from Zoe's face and turns round, and he and Zoe look at Bingy, and so do all the others, and the Hulk says, 'What did you say?' And the Hulk is smiling coldly at the chance of some action in which he'll be the star, and he looks as if he is going to burst out of his T-shirt, like the real Incredible Hulk. He lets go of Zoe and turns and faces Bingy, with his head tilted back on top of his thick neck, and his mouth open, and the rest of them begin smiling and shuffling and they form a sort of semi-circle behind him. Bingy's afraid, but he thinks this is his chance to show Zoe, and he says to the Hulk, 'Just leave her alone, okay,' and he points his finger at him, like it's a gun, and he takes a step forward. The trouble is Bingy is pissed, and he kind of staggers, tripping over his own feet, and they all laugh. And the worst of it is that Zoe laughs too. Bingy looks round, but Spike and Gazz are no-where in sight; not that they would be any use anyway. But this is his chance. 'Zoe,' he says, and he reaches out his arm towards her, 'Are you okay?' He knows enough to be aware that his speech is a bit slurred, but he hopes she'll come forward, take his hand and go off with him toward the bliss he dreams about, leaving them all behind. But she just smiles at him; a sad smile, and she has pity in her eyes and she says, 'Go home, Bingy,' and she shakes her head, and she leans against the Hulk's shoulder, with her hand on his chest and says, 'Just leave him, Finn.' There's some giggling among the others, but Bingy just stands there. He can't just leave, can he? He almost wants the Hulk to hit him, just to show Zoe that he would do anything for her because he loves her so much. After a while, when he hasn't moved, the Hulk comes towards Bingy who clenches his fists, ready, but the Hulk makes a mock jab at him with his own fist and Bingy flinches and turns his head away and closes his eyes, waiting for the blow that doesn't come. And they all laugh and jeer and the Hulk says, 'You're pissed Bingy, just go on home to your granny,' and they all laugh some more, and Bingy feels such a rage he's never known before, like he might explode. And as the Hulk begins to turn back to Zoe, Bingy lunges at him, throwing all the strength he can into his fist, aiming with all his might for the Hulk's grinning face. The curled up fist contains all his love for Zoe and all his jealousy and hate for the Hulk, and he swings so hard and feels triumphant in anticipation of the contact that will come between his knuckles and the Hulk's smug face. But Bingy has never hit anyone before; he's never even tried. A combination of inexperience and inebriation means he misses, his fist swings through fresh air and the force makes him spin and fall, so that he's spread-eagled on the pavement. They all laugh again, and jeer and some of them shout, 'Go home to your granny, Bingy,' like a delayed echo. And then the Hulk comes towards him and towers over him, with his designer trainers next to his face, and Bingy wants him to kick him. He wants the Hulk to smash him; to martyr him for his love for Zoe, but he doesn't. Instead he bends over and takes Bingy's jeans down, and leaves him rolling on the road with them round his ankles, with everyone laughing in a circle around him and Bingy trying to hide himself with his hands.

The Hulk hasn't killed him, or even hurt him, but when he takes his jeans down, it's so much worse and Bingy starts blubbing, and after a while the laughter stops and they all get embarrassed and move away, heading for the pavilion, and leaving him lying on the pavement among the flattened bits of grey chewing gum and the cigarette ends and the spilled grease from the fish suppers. He doesn't notice Zoe looking back at him; he doesn't see her disengage herself from the Hulk's arm which is round her shoulder. He just lies there on his side, trying to pull his jeans back on. The pavement is his whole world just then; a patch of grey damp concrete that will never be clean. He tries to hide himself, but he's in full view, in his best black shirt and jeans that his gran had ironed earlier in the evening. 'Have a good time, love,' she'd said as he left. The staff in Mario's are on tiptoes looking onto the rectangle of yellow light in which he lies, but no-one comes out to see if he's all right. Then old Mrs Reynolds from down the road comes past and says it's disgusting, and Bingy should be ashamed of himself and what would his poor granny say?

Bingy pulls his jeans back on somehow. He needs to get out of the light; he needs to hide away. He doesn't want to go home; he doesn't know what to do, so he goes back to the holly bush down beside the river, glancing in despair at the pathetic images of himself that follow his progress along the street looking back at him through the shop widows. But Spike and Gazz aren't at the holly bush any more; there are just a few twisted empty cans lying in the trampled detritus and dirt. There is some stuff left in one of the cans and he takes a swig. But Gazz must have pissed in it, though Bingy has a couple of swallows before he realises, and he brings it all straight back up and some it it spatters across his black shirt. Then he just sits on the log they carried there for sitting on, sniffing and crying and looking at the black river, and feeling an emptiness that he thinks will always be there. The shower of brightness from the street lights on the bridge illuminates the drizzle and casts slipping discs of silver over the surface of the flowing river, which looks like it is made of oil. The water looks so cold and beautiful and scary, shimmering in the light and slipping away from the town into the darkness of the countryside beyond, and it seems to call him to follow it to the fields beyond where the peewits cry and plunge; to just float away out of town. He picks at a piece of chewing gum that is stuck to his jeans. He pictures his gran ironing them for him for what he said was a date, and after a while he gets up from the log and goes to the edge of the river, and he watches the cold, black, shining water slipping and swirling, and the pools of light playing on its surface. He stands there for what seems ages, suffering from love and humiliation and thinking of everything and nothing. Then he works his way along the bank slipping in the mud and the dog dirt, and when he finds a good place, where the bank isn't too steep, he jumps.

After Bingy hits the water he falls over, and Christ it's cold; it's so cold he cries out. But the water isn't deep and he's able to keep his head up, even though he's lying down. And he looks up and there's a figure on the bridge, framed in the street-lights, and it might be an angel with a halo. And for a moment Bingy wonders if it's Zoe. Then he sees that it's just Mrs Reynolds looking down at him, and she says, 'What are you doing down there, you silly boy? Now get up Richard Bingham, and get yourself home.' And Bingy just says, 'Aye, thanks Mrs Reynolds, I'll do that.' And in a way she's right, because he knows he just needs to get out of the water and get home. So he jogs home to try and get his circulation going. And when he gets there he plans to sneak into the house and go upstairs, but his gran is in the kitchen and when she sees him she looks all concerned and she asks, 'Richard, what on earth have you been doing with yourself?'

He says, 'I fell in the river, Gran, but I'm okay.' And he can't bear her look and he starts crying. He's too cold to take his clothes off by himself, so she does it for him, and he just stands there in the warm kitchen and lets her fiddle with his buttons and his zip, and the smell of her and her touch make him feel better. Then he realises he's lost his phone. He doesn't say anything; his gran had spent so much on it; money she can't afford, and the thought makes him cry again. She runs him a hot bath, and helps him into it because his teeth are chattering and he needs her. He lies for ages in the sweet-smelling foam that she's put in to make him feel better. And later on he comes down in his dressing gown and slippers, and she makes him some hot chocolate, with lots of sugar, and she kisses him on the head, on his hair which is perfumed from the bath, and she doesn't ask him anything. She's already washed his good black shirt and his jeans in the sink, and they are dripping on the clotheshorse, with a carrier bag spread out underneath to catch the water which pats gently against the plastic. They watch telly for a while and later on she says, 'We're a right pair, you and me, Richard.' It's one of those sayings she has that doesn't mean much, but also means lots of things. He smiles at her, and tells her she knows how to make a good mug of hot chocolate.

Later on that night, in bed, Bingy decides he's not ready for love; he tells himself that he's going to wait a bit before getting involved with any more girls. He takes Zoe's crumpled paper tissue from its place under his pillow and after smelling it for one last time he puts it in the bin. And from a drawer in his desk he takes a love poem he'd written for her but never sent. He reads it over:

My love for you is like a shooting star
That travels on and on,
I look after you from afar
Through sunshine wind and rain.
I love you more than you will know,
I love you cos you're you.
And I live in hope that one of these days
You will love me too.

Bingy had been quite pleased with it. But now he tears it into lots of tiny pieces and puts it in the bin, sprinkling it like confetti on top of the tissue. It's over and he's exhausted and soon he sinks into a deep sleep and dreams of swimming, while across town, in the hollowed out holly bush by the river, among the crushed cans and cigarette buts and litter, his phone glows and vibrates over and over as the drizzle forms little rivulets on its surface and seeps into the casing. And on the screen a message flashes: "Zoe calling."

16

Family Man

They have been on their own for twenty-four sleepless hours in which time has become suspended, like the layers of blue cigarette smoke which hang like rainforest mists. The world outside still twists about its axis, humming beyond the closed windows.

Sometimes they pace the floor like tigers, trapped in a stifling cage, not knowing what to do with this time they do not want, unsure whether to fight or mate.

Tyler brings in two mugs of coffee. Ashley stares numbly at the curling steam.

You don't believe her, do you, Ash? He's asked her a hundred times. He extends two cigarettes towards her so she can choose. It's an intimate gesture; unbearable.

I've always wanted to be a family man, Tyler had told them; a declaration of innocence. I love children. He'd been outraged. The police were in plain clothes. The social worker had made her mind up.

Ashley had wanted to slap Jenny. How could she say those things? Fourteen going on nineteen. Out all hours. Covered in love bites. But Jenny was out of reach; after telling her teacher she'd been taken to a home till they could sort things out. It didn't make sense; none of it could be true.

Ashley would have to choose. She already had; she'd signed her child into care. Put her name here and here and here where the social worker had made crosses. Jenny's eyes follow her from the school photo on the TV; a pretty, smiling face captured in better times.

Use the coasters, Ashley says, wearily. She's tried hard to make it homely. Tyson wipes the ring of coffee with his cuff and reaches for a little mat with its red heart design.

She says you used to talk to her through the bathroom door, playing with yourself. She says you would go into her room and lie beside her... The police officer's voice had been calm; dispassionate. Why do you think she would say those things? He sterilised the words as he spoke. Tyson had kept standing up, interrupting. It's disgusting. It's ridiculous. Ashley had been in shock; stunned. She'd had no luck with men until he came along.

The cat jumps onto Tyson's knee, eyes closed, dribbling and thrumming ecstatically from deep within its fur, pressing its claws into his jeans as he absently tickles its ear. Ashley watches his fingers massaging the cat. She's always loved his hands, strong from handling tools, even the tattoos on his knuckles; inscribed with a blade and filled with ink when he was a child. Hands that press and hold her in the night-time.

You don't believe her, do you, Ash?

Ashley can't breathe.

17

The Bogeyman

'You mustn't touch, mind, or the Bogeyman will get you.' Anne's warning to Rory and Flora had been effective for years; humorous at first but more recently darker. She'd never had to explain who or what the Bogeyman was; it was enough to put her finger to her lips and glance from side to side, showing the whites of her eyes.

When they first moved into the house the room had just been called *the front room*; its role was a bit like that of old fashioned parlours; kept tidy for visitors and used occasionally for sitting quietly at teatime on Sundays. Then, as Anne's collection began to take form, Geoff affectionately called it *the museum – her museum*. 'Shall we have our coffee in your museum, love?' And he'd put his arm around her and they'd lean their heads together on the little sofa, after the children had been put to bed, and watch the dancing flames and shadows of the coal-effect gas fire. But, like museums trapped in time that have stuffed animals in glass cases and ancient Chinese vases in display cabinets, it didn't have a long-term future. Now she referred to it as *her room*, and Geoff sneeringly called it *the mausoleum*. He never went in there now; it was as joyless for him as their loveless marriage had become.

When they had been younger Rory and Flora had shared Anne's pleasure, as she carefully lifted and peeled back the sellotape from a white cardboard box, having first picked at it tantalisingly like it was a scab. They'd watch her shining painted nails at work, still carefully manicured in memory of her earlier glamour, topping her now wrinkled fingers, ruined from years of work and motherhood. They had still thought her hands were extensions of them then; as babies they had clenched them in their grasping fists, watching, wide-eyed as the crimson varnish caught flecks of light. Later, they'd found comfort in the sight of them, sparkling through their tears, as she unfolded sticking plasters on their grazed knees after childhood tumbles. The cool, calming touch of her hands had symbolised the essence of the love they automatically exchanged. Then from the box would be drawn the bubble-wrapped shape, and within that the tissue paper, till finally the figurine would be revealed. It was usually a person, a lady perhaps in Victorian dress with a parasol, or dancing, with the cold folds of a pastel coloured dress, swirling, new and perfect, catching shining slippery drops of light that fell in geometric shapes from windows. Sometimes the figure would be an animal: a dog, a cat or a horse, and later, when taste lapsed in favour of less discriminating acquisition, the animal might be clothed. Rory and Flora liked these best of course. 'You mustn't touch, mind,' their mother would always say. 'If you do, the Bogeyman will get you.'

As Rory and Flora grew, the Bogeyman was still close by, even though they now knew he was just a story. He seemed to be outside the door of the bedroom they shared if they talked too late at night, and sometimes at teatime, if they didn't clean their plates. But he seemed closest when they were in the museum.

One day Rory and Flora heard Geoff shouting to Anne that the clothed animals were a ridiculous waste of money. They had taken to shouting at each other often; their relationship had become blistered and painful, like ears of seed trapped between skin and clothes, and they endured their marriage now only for occasional sex, ritual, convenience and of course for the children. The household expenses had gone up for some reason, even though Geoff was working a lot of overtime. At least that's what he told Anne he'd been doing when he came home late; there was little trust between them. The next day Flora asked, 'Doesn't Dad like your ornaments any more, Mam?' But Anne didn't answer; she just looked out of the kitchen window at the line of Geoff's white shirts, still hanging damp and limp in the drizzle, like skins, from the day before.

'Remember to call me Mum, love, Mum, not Mam,' she said after while.

Rory and Flora were torn. When Geoff was out they still sometimes tried to share their mother's pleasure, as she stood admiring her collection. 'These are worth a lot of money, you know: collectors' items, these,' she'd tell them. But the time came when they became weary of her unnecessary reminders to them not to touch anything, and Geoff's disdain for Anne's precious collection had an influence on them. Anne began locking the door and hiding the key, till they stopped wanting to look, even when she had a new figurine to unwrap and display. She changed; she rarely asked about their homework, she made less effort with the cooking and she stopped ironing their clothes. They hardly ever went out as a family any more. Happier times were still captured in framed photographs on shelves: a caravan holiday by the sea and a day trip to the zoo, but it felt a long time ago. Anne's appearance began to alter; she looked far away. Her eyes developed a certain glitter and she became self-absorbed. Her collection of porcelain figures grew steadily. They all moved apart; children and adults; the fissures widening and the angles of their lives twisting, like newly broken ice turning on a stagnant pond.

For years Anne had worked part-time at a supermarket checkout. The pay was poor, but at least the time passed quickly when the store was busy. She used to enjoy the banter: 'Would you like a hand with your packing? We had that gateau last week; it was delicious.' But she chatted less with the customers these days. Sometimes she got free food on its sell-by date as a little perk. It made her feel better about putting a little away for just herself, so she could add to her collection.

Just occasionally Anne wasn't back from work when Rory and Flora got home from school; she couldn't turn down the overtime. The children knew under which stone the backdoor key was hidden, and would let themselves in to the strangely silent and lifeless house, and eat bowls of cereal in front of cartoons. But today Anne had forgotten about Rory's friend, Anurak, who was coming to play after school. Geoff referred to Anurak's parents as *the hippies*. They had painted their fifties tiled fireplace purple and their living room smelled of incense, though Geoff had only been inside once, to extract Rory from an after school visit. Geoff had asked Anurak's parents what the name Anurak meant and when they told him it was Thai for male angel he'd stifled his snigger. It had been an embarrassing moment. Anurak's dad had a ponytail, held in place with a rubber band. His mother wore long Indian skirts with cords of little silver bells, which swung and gently tinkled as she walked. They had six cats, and a stone Buddha on their front step. Anurak was an only child, and his parents allowed him to find out about the world by interacting with it rather than through instruction. He could be like an untrained spaniel let loose among a flock of pheasants. Rory was drawn to him.

On this day, once they were inside the house, Anurak flitted from one thing to another, like a searching hornet. He soon grew bored with the cartoons and frustrated with the computer games, which needed more tenacity than he could muster. He made his way to Rory and Flora's room where he emptied a box of Star Wars figures onto the floor and pulled apart a Lego model that had taken Rory hours to assemble. Rory followed him trying to restore order, and wishing Anne would come home. Flora occasionally appeared, unnecessarily telling Rory that he'd have to tidy up before Mam got back, or he'd get a row.

'What's in here?' asks Anurak, trying the door handle of Anne's room.

Rory was horrified at the question.

'It's just Mam's museum. We're not allowed in.'

Anurak tried the door handle. 'Why's it locked?' The word museum was intriguing, and the locked door held promise.

'It's just Mam's special stuff. Come on. Want a shot with my PlayStation?' Distraction sometimes worked with Anurak.

One moment Anurak was following Rory back to the bedroom, but the next he was gone and the house was oddly quiet. Rory and Flora searched the house together, calling Anurak's name, but apart from sound of the TV there was only a sucking silence.

'He must be hiding,' said Flora. They searched around upstairs, then, coming back downstairs, they saw that the door to the front room was slightly ajar. Rory's heart kicked inside: he just knew something terrible had happened. He pushed at the door gently, Flora at his shoulder. He was trembling. He imagined Anurak in his mother's museum among all the figurines, which would crack if touched, perhaps falling against each other, like a row of unbalanced dominoes. What if the Bogeyman came, he thought, even though he'd known for years that it had always been just an empty threat. Then, as he leaned into the room, reverentially on tiptoes, he sighed with relief. At first glance everything looked normal; the shining, posing figures looked down from the mantelpiece and out from the china cabinet; they stood, flounced and danced as usual in petrified poses on the occasional tables. Anurak was in the middle of the little room with his back to the door, his thin plaited pony tail trailing down his neck.

'You need to come out Anurak,' said Rory, advancing. 'We're not allowed in here. Where'd you find the key anyway?'

But Anurak didn't answer. He turned slowly, displaying the fragments of "Eleanor" in his cupped hands; her dismembered head and arms rolling in his palms. Flora was still at Rory's side. 'That was one of Mum's favourites,' she said, wide-eyed and tragic.

The three children stood for a moment, not knowing what should happen next. 'It's only an ornament,' said Anurak at last. But this was sacrilege, and Rory couldn't stop his eyes filling with tears, for the pain this would cause his mother and for the fear of what she might do. A symbol of her faith had been smashed, like an infidel might destroy a priceless Madonna. An electric current ran down his spine; the Bogeyman was coming.

'I'll get some glue,' said Flora, always the practical one, while Rory removed the pieces from Anurak's cupped hands and led him from the room.

Anurak had gone home before Anne got back from work. She had a cooked chicken and a packet of stir-fry vegetables, with yellow, reduced-sale labels on the packets. She was pleased with the money she'd saved. 'I didn't have to pay for these,' she said, proudly. 'They'd just have been thrown out.' Afterwards the children did the washing up without being asked, and went off to do their homework, unbidden. 'What's got into you two?' she asked, smiling. She was in a good mood. 'I'm going to take my tea into my room and have a quiet sit. I'm so tired.'

She was gone a long time. So long that Flora and Rory eventually went to look for her. She was sitting in the chintz-covered chair she'd inherited from her grandmother, holding the reassembled Eleanor. One of the figurine's arms had become unstuck again. Sellotape held the head grotesquely in place. 'She was one of my favourites,' Anne said. 'You knew that.' She was looking at the pieces, and only the side profile of her head was visible to them from the doorway.

'It was an accident,' began Rory. 'Anurak...'

'Please, just be quiet. Go away the pair of you. Get out of my sight.' The coldness of her tone pierced them like an insect sting.

Later, Anne put the remains of Eleanor in the pedal bin in the kitchen, the pieces lying tragically across the household waste for all to see. She didn't wrap her: she wanted the atrocity to be seen. The inverted image of Eleanor's distorted face glanced back at her as she lifted her foot off the pedal and closed the stainless steel lid. She sat down to wait.

Geoff came home, late and silent. He heated up his dinner in the microwave before sitting down with it on his knee to watch television.

'Where're Rory and Flora?' he asked after a few mouthfuls.

'They've gone to bed.' She kept her eyes on the television.

'Bit early, isn't it?'

'Go and look in the bin.'

'What?'

'Just go and look in the bin.'

Puzzled and weary, Geoff banged down his plate on the floor, so that the fork rolled off onto the carpet. Anne stared at the fork till she heard the familiar squeal of the pedal bin lid being opened and heard Geoff snorting out a laugh through his nose. She looked up at him as he came back into the room.

'Someone's had a smashing time,' he said, grinning. He sat down again, and took up his food.

'Very funny,' Anne said, beginning to sob. 'I get more pleasure from my collection than I do from any of you.' Her hanky was out by now. 'You all just use me as your skivvy. Cooking, cleaning, working. What else is there for me?'

'For Christ's sake, woman, they're plaster. Plaster ornaments.'

'They're porcelain,' she interrupted, correcting him. 'They keep me going.'

'What difference does it make? God knows how much you've spent on them over the years. They're crap and meaningless and ridiculous. Just like you,' he added in an undertone. He kept eating, but the taste had turned to ash.

'God, what's happened to us? Why did I marry you? Sales executive? You're just a jumped up shop assistant like me.' Anne spat out the words between sobs. Her mascara ran down her face in streaks like dark blood.

They looked at each other for a second, each aware of the curious mixture of the familiarity and the distance between them; the intimate knowledge and ignorance of each other, the trail which had led relentlessly to the souring of love and to gathering misery.

The blood rushed to Geoff's face. He could not stifle his hatred any longer: 'Come with me. I'll show you how they bloody break.' He banged his plate of half-eaten dinner back on the floor, the food spinning across the carpet, and stormed out of the room.

'What are you doing, what are you doing?' she screamed, rushing after him in a sudden panic.

He was still in his computer store shirt and tie. He tried the door to the front room but it was locked. 'And it's always bloody locked,' he yelled, his anger further provoked. 'I'll show you, I'll bloody well show you. Watch this.' He pushed his shoulder against the door, twice. It didn't give, and he rubbed at his arm in pain. For some reason she became acutely aware of the balding patch on the back of his head. He thought he saw her smile, contemptuous at his failure. 'Bloody laugh at me would you?' he yelled, and standing back, raised his foot and kicked at the door with the flat of his shoe.

'I wasn't laughing, I wasn't,' she shouted, trying to hold him. 'Stop it, stop it. I'm sorry.'

Again and again and again he kicked, till the plaster around the frame of the door began to crack. Then the door itself splintered around the lock, and with a final kick it gave. Anne was sobbing. 'Stop it, stop it Geoff,' she kept repeating. 'You don't know what you're doing.' He stepped inside, like a great grizzly bear, larger than usual, Anne desperately holding him round the waist. 'No, don't you dare. You can't. Leave them,' she screamed. He grabbed blindly at the ornaments and threw them to the floor. He threw others against the wall; into the fireplace; against each other. She screamed and screamed, clutching at his arms, pulling at his hair, pleading and cursing.

The blow shocked him. The room spun round and he staggered, blood spattering his shirt. His blood. It didn't seem real. She was holding a silver-topped cane; his grandfather's. How could she have hit him with that? He wrenched it from her grasp, though she hardly resisted, shocked herself at what she had done. She backed away, cowering and afraid, but it was over. He stood there for a moment, then went into the hall, collected his jacket and car keys, and still holding the cane, left the house, quietly closing the door behind him, the yale lock clicking as it sealed them apart. She heard him start the car; heard the high pitched whine as he reversed into the road; heard the engine change gear and the sound of it grow faint until it got lost among the traffic.

At the top of the stairs Flora and Rory had watched the scene through the banisters, like the bars of a cage, open-mouthed and silent. When it was over and all that remained was the sound of their mother's sobbing they crept back to bed.

The children got up for school as usual next morning. Anne hadn't put on her make-up and looked strangely pale and ghostly. They knew Geoff wasn't around, but Flora had to ask.

'Where's Dad?'

'He had to go to work early today. Eat your breakfast or you'll be late for school.'

'I'm sorry about your ornament, Mum,' said Rory. 'I'll save up and get you another one.'

Anne didn't say anything.

The children put their packed lunches (rolls and ham with expired best-before dates) into their school-bags and quietly left the house together.

Anne didn't work late that evening. She had something special for tea: crispy aromatic quarter duck. The store didn't buy in many and she was lucky there had been one left. There wasn't enough for everyone, but Rory and Flora could have beans on toast; they liked that. She laid the table herself. Rory and Flora usually took turns to do this, but they hadn't come home yet. Neither had Geoff. Later, when they still weren't home she ate alone. She tried Geoff's mobile, but just got put through to his voicemail, and couldn't bring herself to speak. She assumed the children were with him. The duck was a disappointment and after picking at it she put it in the bin, in which the pieces of Eleanor still lay. The sauce dribbled over the shattered remains. She took her tea, in a Spode china cup and saucer, to her room. Earlier she'd cleared away the mess. A few ornaments had survived: the broken ones were in a cardboard box in the corner. She knew they were destroyed beyond repair, but she didn't know what to do with them; they felt like the remains of her life. The surviving figurines were spread around the room; a ballerina here, an elephant with its calf there.

Her cup was half way to her lips when she saw them: two porcelain children, from the German Hummel factory, fused together, hand in hand. They were on the mantelpiece. She'd never seen them before. She put down her tea and moved closer, her jaw slack. They had the manufacturer's design trademark of innocent expression and the hand-painted orange hue that she loved so much. She looked closer and gasped: there was no doubt; they were *her* children; Flora and Rory smiling out at her in fine detail, in the school uniforms they had gone out in that morning, with their schoolbags slung on their backs. They were walking away from her, looking over their shoulders, each giving her a smile and a wave.

18

The Exorcism

Coriander had been planning the exorcism for weeks. After walking for about forty-five minutes through the awakening city, still cranking into life with the whining of bus engines and the hiss of their brakes, in a clinging haar, she reached the Royal Park and began ascending the path that runs along a broad ledge under the crags, near the famous volcanic plug of Arthur's Seat. She hadn't been there ages, but the uncomfortable memory of her father's route-marches when she had been a child broke upon her within yards of her setting foot upon its rust-coloured, crumbling surface. Come on, keep up, Margaret. There had been no time to stand and stare and no sympathy for the blisters that formed in her wellyboots. As soon as she went off to University she'd changed her name and went home only at Christmas, but his sarcasm and inability to love anything had bruised her for ever.

Dedicated joggers pounded past her in both directions; the women's sinewy arms pumping and their breasts rising and falling inside their tight tops. Men pushed themselves till they were soaked in sweat. She kept her eyes on the path. A muscular man in a singlet closed a nostril with the knuckle of his index finger and violently discharged a plug of mucous as he veered around her on his descent. She glanced at it, spreading and glistening across a cold stone. She took everything personally.

Soon Edinburgh was unrolling below her: the grey details opening out, but unfocused and dissolving in the middle distance, consumed by the mists. The path curved under the moody crags, and soon she reached a place where the ledge broadened out and some large boulders afforded a measure of privacy and shelter. The sounds of the city were distant and muffled. She could have been on a remote hillside; on Macbeth's blasted heath. Double double toil and trouble, she muttered aloud, smiling to herself. A good day for an exorcism. A gentle breeze was stirring and she enjoyed its cool brush against her cheek. She looked about her, then crouched in the lee of the rocks, took a small tartan rug from her rucksack and spread it on the ground. She sat on the rug, conflicted. She slowly relaxed when it became clear that the passing joggers who trickled by were oblivious or indifferent. She wondered at their energy, at their strength, their single-mindedness. She could never go out in public looking like that. She did some breathing exercises for a few moments, then adopted the nearest thing she could to a lotus position. It wasn't comfortable; despite lots of practise she still found it difficult to sit cross-legged for very long and would never be able to get her feet above her knees. It was hard to concentrate, she felt so exposed in the great out-doors. She took a plastic bag from her rucksack, and from this removed a length of string, which she passed through her fingers. Then she began to tie knots in the string: one knot for each of her warts.

She began whispering, 'With these knots my warts I shall vanquish,' This part hadn't been on the websites she'd pored over, but she felt the need to articulate something aloud. She repeated the words for each knot she tied, and when they were all prepared she set the prose to a harmony that came to her at the moment, and transformed it to a poetic prayer, still whispering. 'With these knots my warts I shall vanquish, with these knots my warts I shall vanquish, vanquish, vanquish.'

'Are you okay missus?' A boy in a grubby white T-shirt was standing a few feet away. His hand was inside his trousers, scratching.

The voice, unexpected and close, made Coriander jump and cry out like one of the wheeling gulls. She quickly shoved everything back into her bag and stood up, her pale face burning a deep shade of pink and her neck breaking out in blotches.

'Sorry, I didn't mean to make ye jump. Only I thought you might have hurt yersel; all that rockin about and mutterin and stuff.' He paused for a moment then looked towards the rolling, grey clouds, tumbling overhead. 'Folk sometimes jump off thae cliffs up there. Folk who aren't right in the heid.'

The colour in Coriander's face deepened. She followed the line of his eye up the face of the crags that reached over them, and for a moment the quickly passing clouds gave the illusion that the towering cliffs were falling slowly down upon them. Their eyes met; they each seemed to know that they had experienced the same thrill. The boy had stopped scratching himself, and was now biting his fingernails; nibbling a corner, pausing to examine the result, then chewing again.

They turned to face the city and stood for a while in silence. The iron-grey cloud seemed to flow like lava, smothering the place. There were a few spots of rain.

'Poor things.' Coriander's voice was thin and tremulous. She thought of people floating through the rushing air for a few seconds before being extinguished on the rocks below. She wondered if they closed their eyes. She wondered if they changed their minds after taking the final leap.

'Not the way I'd choose to go if you was to ask me. One of my old teachers did it wi a bottle of whiskey and some pills. That's more like it, I'd say. What do you think? Except I can't abide the whiskey. I'd go for vodka I think, and some of me ma's pills, that's what I'd choose, they seem to make her happy. I'd want to go happy, that's if I was thinking of it, you understand.'

Coriander nodded. The boy seemed to make it all sound as simple and everyday as infusing green tea.

According to Coriander's research the exorcism had to be carried out in a suitable outdoor location, ideally a cemetery. She'd done some fieldwork: she'd stood for a time among the slanting headstones in the ancient graveyard near her flat, eyeing their carved skulls and crossed bones, and she'd looked at the lifeless, cold eyes of white marble angels, smeared green with microscopic plant life. But it was just too close to death; so close she could smell it. She'd thought hard about alternatives. She even wondered about the stark, neglected back green of her tenement, with its sunless and austere qualities, but the surrounding windows had stared blankly down on her, hiding prying eyes, and as she'd strolled about she'd stepped on a plastic phallus, presumably thrown from one of them, and now waiting in the damp, uncut grass. Then she'd come up with the idea of Salisbury Crags; the ragged stone curtain of volcanic rock below Arthur's Seat, with an easily accessible footpath. She'd remembered a story about a series of miniature coffins having been found in a cave there and had decided that the place would supply the right ambience for her operation.

'Poor things,' she said again, 'To get into that hopeless state.'

'Aye. Radge if you ask me. Apparently about ten folk jump off the Forth road bridge every week, but they hush it up cos they dinnae want tae give others the same idea. That's why there's no footpath on the new one - Queensferry Crossing. You know Russia has the highest suicide rate in the world. And Syria has the smallest. Hard to believe isn't it?'

'You seem to know a lot.' Coriander's blushes were subsiding.

'I did a project at school. You could choose anything.'

'Have you heard about the coffins they found here?' asked Coriander. The boy shook his head. 'Well, in the 1830s some boys were hunting for rabbits and they came across a wee cave that contained seventeen miniature coffins, about four inches long, each with a tiny wooden figure inside, with a pained face and clothes. The coffins were decorated with metal. You can see them in the museum. Some people think they were spells of death made by witches wanting to destroy their enemies, but I think they were part of an ancient custom of burying likenesses of people who had died in faraway lands. That's a much nicer story.'

'Cool. I like the witches story the best. I wonder if it would work on some of the folk I know. I wouldn't mind getting rid of some of them!'

Coriander looked at him

'Only joking,' he laughed. 'What's all that stuff ye got?' He moved closer and picked up Coriander's knotted string, which had fallen on to the grass. 'Hey this is cool'.

'Be careful with it,' pleaded Coriander. His hands were dirty, and she feared that he might sully the string and spoil her chances of success.

'Aye, you're all right, here you go.' He handed back the string. 'So what is it yer tryin tae do?' He began picking at particles of crusty mucous in his nostrils.

Coriander was wary of children. She'd been uncomfortable about them even when she was a child herself. They were too open and honest, uninhibited and cruel. She sometimes crossed the road to avoid groups of them eating their sandwiches and chips during their school lunch breaks, jostling with each other and throwing their packaging about. Some of them seemed to sense her fear and called her names from across the street. This one seemed different, despite his close-cropped hair and the stud in his ear. She felt a curious connection. She thought he must be about twelve. The breeze billowed out his T-shirt from his skinny body, and he smiled at her with inviting openness. He must be freezing, she thought. The breeze had increased and the haar was lifting. It had seemed so still at the foot of the hill.

'Shouldn't you be going to school?' she asked. You always asked children about school, didn't you?

'I'll go later. Special timetable. They say I'm on the spectrum. Shouldn't you be at your work?'

'I'm retired, medically retired. They say I'm on the spectrum too! You mustn't let them label you,' she added.

'What d'you mean?'

'Categorising you. Putting you in a box. Telling you there's something wrong about you, something different.'

'It's okay,' he says. 'I get a special timetable and my ma gets an allowance. PIP they call it. She needs it. Especially with that dickhead who's moved in with her. Really fancies hisself. Trains with his weights in front of the mirror and stuff. You have to watch him, though, he killed someone once; did eight years inside. They should've thrown away the key if ye ask me. He's always shovin me off the computer so's he can play. An he's crap anyway.' It all sounded so matter of fact. 'So what's the string for eh?'

Coriander dangled the string between her delicate fingers like a daisy chain. 'I'm here to perform an exorcism.'

The boy seemed unsurprised. 'That's funny, cos I'm here for the exercisin an all. Wi the dug, Jack. In fact where is the bugger?' He looked around him then wandered off down the path, shouting and whistling for the dog as he went.

Coriander watched him go. She was a bit sorry. Talking with the boy had somehow given her confidence. All the knots had to be burned away so that her warts would disappear. It sounded ridiculous, she knew. But what was so different between that and believing in a god, or for that matter in giving your husband peace by burying a likeness of him in a miniature coffin? At this stage in her life she'd decided nobody really knew anything for certain. She'd tried everything else, but the warts seemed to thrive. They were like limpets, sucking the life juices from her and blooming all over her fingers. She set to work, but although she managed to light some matches, they blew out almost immediately. She huddled against a boulder, trying to create sufficient shelter, but match after match flared briefly, like a tantalising arc of hope, then died, and she sank down in despair. The drops of rain fell more quickly.

'Hello again. Havin trouble?' The boy had returned, this time with his dog; a large hairy mongrel, which sat down and began scratching ecstatically at its neck, stretching its jaw so that it seemed to smile. It approached Coriander, its tail wagging and its tongue lolling. She leaned away.

'Don't worry about Jack. He wouldn't hurt a fly; unless I told him to of course.'

From her kneeling position she warily extended an arm and patted the dog's head. Jack pressed himself against her and she tumbled over on the grass.

'Away ye go Jack,' the boy shouted, raising an arm as if to strike the animal.

'No, no, he's fine,' said Coriander, but the dog had moved away.

'I think he likes you,' said the boy. Jack stood there looking at them before cocking a leg at a boulder and squeezing out a trickle of urine. They watched it as it sniffed among the grass. The boy took the string from Coriander and studied it.

'I have to burn the knots away, you see,' she explained. 'To exorcise my warts.'

He turned the string over in his hands, and looked at her quizzically, but he didn't seem to need further explanation. 'Ye can borrow ma lighter if ye like.' He produced a cigarette lighter from his pocket, and to show what kind of man he was he lit a crumpled cigarette, effectively cupping his hands against the wind. He saw the look she gave him, and said in a reassuring tone, 'It's okay, I'm tryin tae cut down.'

'I used to smoke myself, once,' she said, with a trace of pride.

Coriander's initial instinct to reject the boy's offer of help was checked by the undeniable effectiveness with which he'd lit his cigarette, despite the breeze. 'Well if you're sure you don't mind,' she said, after a brief internal struggle. He accepted it all without question, as if he came across these problems every day.

'Nae bother.' He handed her the lighter, but although she managed to produce a flame for a couple of seconds it made little impression on the knotted string. 'Here, let me give it a try, he said. 'Hold this for a bit.' He took a long draw on his cigarette before handing it to her, then took the lighter and string from her and huddled against the rock. After some effort he managed to blacken the string. He looked up at her. 'Here, come and help me shelter it.' She crouched down beside him, holding the cigarette aloft. Their shoulders were touching. He blackened the string a bit more. She could feel the warmth of his body and smell the tobacco smoke that still clung to him and blew around them.

'A ken what we'll dae.' He tampered with the lighter in a way that released some of the fuel onto the string, then applied the flame to it once again. One by one the knots fell apart, and soon there were just a few short lengths of charred string. He leapt to his feet. 'Heh heh,' he shouted, laughing. 'Who's the boss, who's the king?'

'You are,' laughed Coriander. She looked down at her warts and rubbed her hands together.

The boy danced about with his arms in the air. 'The king is *in* the house, the king is *in* the house,' he shouted.

A jogger passing by a few feet away nearly fell over.

They looked at each other in triumph, both smiling in the afterglow of success. Both the boy's and Coriander's fingers were blackened with fingering the charred string, and the boy had a small burn on his forefinger which he now sucked then shook.

'Let me see,' Coriander said.

'It's nothin,' he said, but she insisted on applying some calendula ointment, which she produced from her rucksack. Their hands became entwined as she gently massaged in the ointment, until it was absorbed into the grimy whorls of his fingertip. The boy noticed the warts on Coriander's fingers for the first time. 'You should get thae things taken off,' he said. 'Kevin had one on his nose and the doctor gave him some acid stuff which burned it off quick as a jiffy.'

Coriander looked into the boy's eyes.

'Ye've got a nice smile,' he said.

Coriander laughed. 'So have you.'

The lighter was plainly broken, having been sacrificed for the exorcism. Coriander offered to pay for a replacement. 'Dinnae be daft,' said the boy, 'I can easy nick another.' The dog had disappeared again. 'I need tae go,' he said. 'See ye again, maybe. 'My name's Benny, by the way,' he said. And he offered her his hand. Coriander held out her own hand, which, for a moment, hung in the air like a dead herring.

'Coriander,' she said.

He grasped her cold, limp fingers and gave her hand a firm shake.

'Pleased to meet you. Enjoy your exercisin.' He wandered off, shouting, 'Jack, Jack, come here you bugger.'

'Thank you, Benny,' Coriander called after him, giving him a wave.

'Nae bother, Coriander,' Benny returned.

Coriander sat for a while, enjoying the grey drizzle. Then she carefully packed up her things in the rucksack and began picking her way back down the path. The gossamer-like haar had nearly cleared and there were gaps of blue sky showing through the breaking cloud. As she descended back towards the city she caught the eye of a jogger. 'Morning,' she said impulsively with a smile.

'Hiya,' the woman panted back.

19

Evensong

The day Daniel Laidlaw was chosen to be head chorister was one of the happiest days of his father's life. It had all been worth it; not just the fees for the choir school, but the early starts to get Daniel to choir practice before school each morning; collecting him each evening after evensong; giving up lazy Sundays and indulgent Christmases so that he could be taken to and from services to sing in the choir. The miles they had clocked up! The hours they had devoted to the cause of sacred music! But now here he was: head chorister, with the silver medal of this high office round his neck, leading the choir and singing solos. What a voice! Could anything be more beautiful? There was talk of producing a CD. The Chichester Psalms, maybe. The proud father had been to every service since his son's elevation the previous week and now sat in the centre of the nave, looking ahead with an inner, satisfied smile that just reached his lips. To crown his sense of everything being well with the world Jim Laidlaw had earlier secured a lucrative deal that could clinch his promotion. He was glowing.

The sparse congregation was scattered about in the enormous space. Each worshipper seemed to want to be as far away as possible from everyone else. Jim Laidlaw recognised one or two faces. There were other chorister-parents of course, though most would arrive towards the end of the service to collect their children. Afterwards they will gather outside the room where the children changed back into their school clothes, and nod to each other and sometimes gossip; there was a surprising amount of politicking associated with the choir and the cathedral. One or two stayed in their cars outside, some with the engine running, filling the air with toxicity as they listened to the news, dozed or even smoked.

Jim Laidlaw knew other members of the congregation by sight; a man in the next row occasionally dropped in clutching a briefcase and Jim speculated that he came to listen to evensong before going home from work. Near the front, Miss McGeowan knelt on a hassock, dutifully embroidered with an image of St Baldred by someone now forgotten. Her eyes were tightly closed and her pinched, floury face was ringed by a mauve beret, like a slipped halo. Jim Laidlaw had talked to her once, but her loneliness depressed him so he now avoided her.

After over fifty years of prayer she was still a virgin, almost friendless and forgotten by her surviving relatives. To the side of the cathedral sat a younger man, a stranger, a bit scruffy. He had been off drugs for a couple of days now. He used the back of his hand to wipe a drop of watery mucous from the end of his nose. He pressed his fists against his eyes and shuddered convulsively, his greasy hair trembling against his knuckles. Who knew how or why he'd found himself there? Why any of them had for that matter. Or, maybe more curiously, why more people had not discovered this special time in a special place. There was a thin scattering of about a dozen others at the service. The tiny congregation took their seats and the master of the music carved through the air with his pale, waxy hands, his white surplice billowing about him as he conducted.

Daniel Laidlaw's voice was vulnerable but sure, hanging in the air for a moment, before being followed by the basses, descants and tenors, each trailing their exquisite pathways of sound, written down five hundred years earlier by Byrd. High up a shard of crimson glass, anchored by cold, grey lead in the Palozi window, buzzed faintly, discordant and unheard. A few of the scattering of worshippers rose as the choir sang for the Glory of God, discomforting those who did not know the rules, then they sank to the stone flags in silence for prayers. Daniel's big moment would come soon; a challenging solo which he'd practised over and over. It brought a tear to his father's eye; there was something about the fragility of the child's treble voice, innocent yet on the brink of manhood.

The felt-lined door, itself within the massive West door, opened periodically to admit a chorister-parent or sometimes head-turning tourists, who wandered around the outer aisles, observing, rehearsing the postcards they would later write, or taking photographs, though the sign said this was forbidden during services. As the door opened, in briefly would seep, like gas, the busy noise of traffic and the city, followed by a thud; the visitors hardly ever read the sign to close the door quietly. A few night-lights flickered in front of an image of Our Lady with the baby Jesus, throwing around melancholic shadows of memories and sorrows. The music echoed in the vaulting space, built in the Gothic style in a different age by hungry men in cotton and corduroy, with mallets and trowels, some killed in the process and all now turned to dust and forgotten. The cathedral was not in the same league as Durham or York; it did not have the same ancient tradition that had been weathered by time; nor had it imbibed the faith of countless generations. But it still took away the breath when visitors looked up to gaze into its lofty heights.

In the choir-stalls, during the reading from the Old Testament, two choristers played paper, scissors, stone; an occasional slap and a suppressed cry was just discernible to the master of the music, who frowned in the direction of the row of the prepubescent descants, upon whom all this ritual for adults depended. Behind them one of the lay clerks, prematurely balding, with a goatee to compensate, was desperate for a cigarette, and musing whether he could be bothered with Ellie's party that night, and another asked himself what he would do now that his girlfriend was pregnant, and he wondered if she'd planned it. Already he resented the child, for whom he would almost certainly have to abandon his PhD, which lay in hopeless piles of foolscap around their flat.

Into all this stepped Jodie and Sam, giggling and loud. Bored, maybe, or hiding from something or someone, or just exploring. The door banged behind them as they intruded into the service with a rush of draughty autumnal energy. Outside the air was alive and the wind had whipped through their hair and made the loosened red cherry leaves dance and rush, but inside the cathedral the trapped, stale atmosphere, scented with incense, felt stifling to the girls and they uttered a wordless cry of surprise. They looked about them, twisting their heads like newly caged birds, briefly in awe of the world in which they found themselves. Jodie's dark, wavy hair, which she hated, turned on her freckled face, and Sam's fine, straight fair hair, envied by Jodie, shone like liquid. One or two heads turned as the girls scraped their chairs on the stone flags and talked in light mercurial tones, the awe they initially felt quickly vaporising. They were as close as friends could be; they found humour and joy and mischief in everything and in nothing. They wore similar clothes, they copied each other's behaviour, they fed off each other's laughter and knew instinctively what each other was feeling. They had a bond that was closer than anything either of them would ever experience again. Together they were taking on the world.

The choir rose to sing the psalm, the carefully enunciated words lifting and falling in the choristers' reedy, virginal voices, which were shortly joined by the men's bass tones, as the organ trembled and shook the air. Sam's phone jangled a downloaded tune and she scrambled to answer it as she and Jodie fell against each other, collapsing into unsuppressed laughter. 'I wouldn't go out with you if you was the last boy on planet earth, Tyson Ferguson,' shouted Sam into her phone and she hung up. The phone jangled again almost immediately. The girls continued to mutter in stage whispers, heads down, as the psalm drew to a close. As the choristers sat down after the psalm they dug each other in the ribs and sniggered, wondering what the fearsome Mr Halswell-Stewart, the choirmaster, would do. But it was the verger, not the choirmaster who intervened. He worked his way apprehensively along the row of chairs, (the uncomfortable pews had been removed years before) trying to look authoritative.

'I'm sorry girls, but you'll need to be quiet or I'll have to ask you to leave,' he whispered.

'We're not doing anything,' said Jodie, loudly, so that everyone could hear.

'Okay, just be quiet, all right?' He backed away and they watched him go. As soon as he was gone they broke down into barely stifled peals of laughter, bent down behind the seats. A few heads turned to look at them; Miss McGeowan was unsettled and Jim Laidlaw was getting angry; Daniel's solo, his big moment, was approaching.

The verger returned. 'Now girls, I'm warning you...'

'Piss off,' said Jodie.

'Yes, bugger off,' echoed Sam.

'There's no need for that,' he said. 'You just need to be quiet, okay?' He backed away and returned, red faced, to his office at the back of the cathedral. This wasn't in his job description.

There was more giggling and whispering from the girls. 'Go on, I dare you.'

So Sam blew a raspberry, barely audible at first, then Jodie blew a slightly louder one. The trumpeting farty noises became louder and the giggling became more hysterical. More suppressed sniggering broke out among the choristers; they had never experienced anything like it; they did not know whether to be shocked or amused. It was revolutionary; their world was normally so ordered and disciplined: choir practice at eight in the morning and again at four in the afternoon after school, and sung services five days a week. There couldn't be a greater contrast to these girls, who seemed to follow no rules. Some of the younger choristers were given warning taps on the shoulder by the lay clerks behind who whispered to them to shush.

The vice-provost had learned to address a congregation of five hundred worshippers; the cathedral was filled to overflowing at Christmas, but the intimate impertinence of the girls baffled him and he did not know what to do. He had been appointed because of his youth and energy; a small jewelled earring shone with a blue sparkle in his left lobe. He carried on with the service, thinking he would speak to the girls afterwards; reach out to them. The provost sat opposite him, passive in this service, but watching. Maybe this was an opportunity, thought the vice-provost, a test? He led the credo, singing in a high monotone, a caricature of a priest, despite his earring.

'I believe in the Holy Ghost.'

The girls interjected; cutting across the responses of the choir and the congregation. 'I don't believe in ghosts, do you Jodie?'

'Oh Lord save the queen'

'With all her money she can save herself.'

'Lighten our darkness we beseech thee oh Lord'

'Why don't you use electric lights like the rest of us?'

'Defend us from all perils of this night.'

'Aye, especially from me mam's boyfriend.' They cackled with laughter at this.

The vice-provost stopped singing and the spoken prayers began. Still the girls interrupted, sure now that they were untouchable.

'And we pray for all who are in need. For those who watch and wait this night.'

'Aye me mam will be watching and waiting,' called Sam.

'And for the victims of the Asian earthquake.'

'What about the starving bairns in Africa?'

The vice-provost halted for a moment, then glanced towards the girls.

'Yes and for those who have nothing to eat in Sudan and Malawi.'

'What about India?'

'And for children in need all over the world.'

'Aye, I could do with a big mac maself.'

The verger came along again. 'Come on, you two, you'll have to leave.'

'Lay one finger on me and I'll scream,' said Jodie.

He bent forwards.

'Rape!' The word rang out through the stale air, echoing through every corner of the great cathedral. The service came to a halt.

'Suit yourselves, I'm going to call the police.'

'It's all right Mr Proudfoot,' the provost called from the front. He had risen to his feet. The vice-provost looked at him, his face colouring.

'Aye piss off Proudfoot,' sneered Sam.

The verger was very flustered. He backed off again.

It was all too much for some. The man with the briefcase got up and crept down the side aisle to escape, unnoticed. Miss McGeowan crossed herself and she too quickly made her exit. She was plainly upset, but the girls seemed impervious. The man with the runny nose looked at Jodie and Sam, smiling; admiring something about them. Jim Laidlaw thought the verger was a fool. In the confusion the choirmaster, Mr Halswell-Stewart, took control: he rose and the anthem began. It was a new piece, commissioned by the cathedral from an up and coming composer. It had a high treble part which Daniel had been practising at home. It was his big moment. He raised his head waiting for his cue, waiting to sing his solo for which he seemed to have been preparing all his life. At a look from Mr Haswell-Stewart his voice rose in the air, unsuspecting, like a doomed linnet. The girls couldn't believe it. 'He sings like a girl!' they shrieked, and they snorted and giggled, fiddling with their phones to catch the moment. Daniel's voice faltered and broke, and he croaked a few notes before ceasing altogether. His place in the world shattered along with his voice; his brief career as a soloist was over. The choristers gasped with sympathy and horror; their voices were the centre of their lives and they felt Daniel's tragedy and loss. The master of the music glared at the girls and Jim Laidlaw rose to his feet in a fury, ready to tear them apart. He began advancing towards them, only to stop halfway. The organ fell silent and the only sound was their indistinct chatter. This was their show. They were standing, holding the gaze of the choir, the clergy and what was left of the congregation. They were chewing bubblegum, opening and closing their mouths in challenging insolence. Sam worked her gum around her mouth and blew a large defiant bubble. It swelled until it burst with a gentle explosion across her face, and she gathered up the pink splattered fragments with her tongue and drew them back unto her mouth. Then Jodie did the same. There was no giggling now; they were defiant, triumphant and unreachable. After a moment they turned and walked slowly down the central aisle towards the rear of the cathedral. When they reached the door they turned and glared defiantly towards the altar, each raising two fingers which they waved in a gesture towards the tableau of people staring at them before passing through the door, which closed with a bang as a gust of lonely November air blew around the entrance area, spinning a few dried out leaves and fluttering some leaflets about Fair Trade.

There was a pause till the vice-provost said, 'May the peace of God go with you.' The provost stared at him in disbelief.

The organ started, and the choir rose. Daniel Laidlaw took up the shining silver cross, which glittered through his oozing tears, and the clergy and choir, followed by the master of the music, filed out as the organist played a Bach fugue.

The verger and the provost remained behind. 'Sorry about that Michael,' said the verger. 'Never known anything like it. I'll stand by the door next time.'

'No, it's all right, John,' said the provost. He went over to where the girls had been sitting and he straightened the chairs. He picked up a bubble gum wrapper from the floor. The organ fell silent at last; Bach dying away in the dusty, dark corners. The cathedral had never seemed so empty.

20

Fishing

We knew nothing about fishing. I'd never liked the idea of putting wriggling white maggots on hooks; of killing, of violence. Even towards fish; no fur nor feathers and cold as if not really alive, but living nonetheless. But you'd seen that man land a fish on the pier and you gave me no peace until I agreed to buy a rod. Besides, something to do together, I thought. Some quality time. It was a family joke: QT with Dad. But it was important; something to do together before you no longer wanted to go fishing with your dad. At £20 a good investment.

We snared our clothes as we climbed the barbed wire fence; I held the twisting top down while you stepped over with your boy's legs, not yet long enough to escape snagging. We both laughed, *nearly caught something already*, I joked, and let the wire go after you had climbed over. It straightened with a squeal, the waves of sound singing. We slid down the bank, arms waving to keep our balance, stumbling in potholes of stagnant water and festering seaweed from the last spring tide, then along the margin between land and sea, till we reached the rocks; cold, black and glistening, thrown from a volcano in a time not possible to conceive. Out to sea a single gannet plunged, folding its wings like a collapsing umbrella just before making contact with the rumpled surface.

We had just the one rod, with its lure and hook to deceive and kill. The man in the shop had said we didn't need bait, not for mackerel. You flicked the guard on the spool and cast into the Sound like he'd showed you, the line zinging through the air at your first attempt. *Yea, go go go,* I shouted. You were so sure of success. But the line became snagged among the seaweed at the first cast and had to be cut loose. We huddled in the sea-soaked breeze and you tied another hook. At this rate these would be expensive fish!

We took turns with the single rod, under the slate-grey sky that threatened rain, but held back; it was my birthday! This is a gift, I thought, as I watched you, my son. So hard to believe; *my son.* Something to treasure, but not to say out loud.

It always looked as if the fishing might be better farther on. We moved over the jagged rocks, disturbing the oyster catchers, dressed to kill, with their beating wings and piping cries, and the circling curlews with their piercing calls. Then, suddenly the rod curved and the line went tight; you landed a pollack, silver and trembling, after it had swung through the air, twisting on the hook. Between us, trembling too, we removed the hook and released it back; too small to eat, too young to die. We watched as it trailed leaking blood, sinking into the heaving, breathing sea, its pulsing, slippery wetness lingering on our cold hands.

We'd told the others that we wouldn't need the pizzas; we'd bring back fish for tea. But time was running out. Then at last, when it seemed the light would fade and we'd have to go back empty handed, a mackerel stretched the line and we felt its quivering fear. You bore it home in triumph in a Tesco carrier through the oncoming darkness, and this time vaulted the fence without my help. You had grown in a couple of hours! We left two trails of trodden grass, side by side, as we crossed the field, the cottage lights already falling upon the sloping ground, guiding us towards the end of our time together. Seeds from the feathery stems and yellow petal-discs of buttercups stuck to our boots as we swished through the wind-blown grass. Over our shoulders the gannet dived for one last time.

You gutted the mackerel using your new Swiss army knife. I watched you, amazed at what you'd become in what seemed no time at all, since I held you against my skin as a newborn. The blue-black shining mackerel, with its wavy patterns of spots and dashes, like the sea it had known, was folded inside sheets of foil, like a shroud, and baked with herbs. We shared it with the others; a flaky mouthful each, pulled from a forest of kelp. *Best fish ever* I said, and you smiled. That smile you've always had; that smile you have kept in the intervening years and have given now to your baby son.